"I Suppose This Deal Needs At Least A Handshake."

"To seal it?"

"At the very least." Brian's hand swallowed Sydney's, then let it slip away. Before Sydney had a chance to react, Brian wrapped his arm around her and pulled her close. "Actually, a handshake won't quite do it. We're talking major agreement here. After all, I may lose my job over this."

Sydney looked up, but he was so close that she could barely see him. "Your job?" she murmured softly as a delicious medley of sensations seemed to float around her. His dark head was backlighted by the sun, but she could see the half smile, sensual and tempting, as he nodded.

"And a deal's a deal once it's sealed," Brian said with satisfaction as he lowered his head to close the remaining inch of space between them.

Dear Reader:

Welcome! You hold in your hand a Silhouette Desire—your ticket to a whole new world of reading pleasure.

A Silhouette Desire is a sensuous, contemporary romance about passions, problems and the ultimate power of love. It is about today's woman—intelligent, successful, giving—but it is also the story of a romance between two people who are strong enough to follow their own individual paths, yet strong enough to compromise, as well.

These books are written by, for and about every woman that you are—wife, mother, sister, lover, daughter, career woman. A Silhouette Desire heroine must face the same challenges, achieve the same successes, in her story as you do in your own life.

The Silhouette reader is not afraid to enjoy herself. She knows when to take things seriously and when to indulge in a fantasy world. With six books a month, Silhouette Desire strives to meet her many moods, but each book is always a compelling love story.

Make a commitment to romance—go wild with Silhouette Desire!

Best,

Isabel Swift
Senior Editor & Editorial Coordinator

SALLY GOLDENBAUM
Honeymoon Hotel

Silhouette Desire

Published by Silhouette Books New York

America's Publisher of Contemporary Romance

SILHOUETTE BOOKS
300 East 42nd St., New York, N.Y. 10017

ISBN: 0-373-05423-8

First Silhouette Books printing May 1988

SALLY GOLDENBAUM

Born in Wisconsin, Sally now lives in Missouri, where she has been successfully writing contemporary romance novels for the past five years, as well as teaching at the high school and college level. Married for almost twenty years, Sally also holds a master's degree in philosophy and has worked both as a textbook writer and as a public relations writer for public television.

One

Sydney Hanover pushed her way past two burly looking men in plaid shirts and slipped onto an empty chair near the back of the crowded room. A hazy blur of blue cigar smoke circled her head, and she made a feeble attempt to wave it away.

"Have I missed much?" she whispered above the auctioneer's quick voice, as he rolled off a description of an old carriage.

"Not too awfully much, dear," answered Lida Jacobs, the plump, pleasant-looking lady seated next to her. "But the cows are all gone."

"Oh, Lida, can you imagine what Grams would do if I brought her home a cow?" Sydney crossed her blue-jeaned legs and laughed. "She'd name it first, probably—"

"Then bake it some buttermilk biscuits, no doubt," Lida chimed in, waving her plump hand through the air. "I sure can imagine. And then she'd bed it down in one of her guest rooms on that pretty linen of hers!"

The auctioneer's gavel added an exclamation mark to Lida's words as he cemented another sale.

"So I missed the cows. What else?"

"Outdoor stuff, mostly. The inn furnishings won't go on the block until tomorrow."

"Tomorrow?" Sydney grimaced. "I guess I'll have to come back. Grams has me looking for an old Tiffany lamp she thinks was in the bridal suite on her honeymoon."

Lida laughed. "Doesn't that sound just like Hortense!"

"I'll have to ask Gus about it, I guess," Sydney said, half to herself.

"Oh, dear." Lida sat up straighter in the hard wooden chair, and her gray brows drew together unhappily. "I guess the big attraction is next—selling the inn."

Sydney nodded, then patted Lida's arm comfortingly. "Poor Gus. It must kill him to sell this place."

"Oh, selling it is a fact of life, dearie. We all get old, y'know. It's the other tragedy that has his stomach churnin' sour." She shook her head and tisked loudly over the din.

"The other?" Sydney lifted her brows, but Lida had turned her attention to the auctioneer, who was pounding dramatically on the high oak table and sending flurries of dust into the air.

"Ladies and gents," the bald man bellowed. "Now is the big moment, the r-e-a-l-l-y big moment," he added, stretching out the word extravagantly.

The crowd seemed to sit up straighter, and the noise muted to an expectant, charged hush.

"It's time to auction the Candlewick Inn itself, this lovely old inn situated here in the middle of these rolling Vermont hills with a half hundred luscious acres of maple trees begging for you to tease the sweetness out of them."

Sydney moaned. Why did auctioneers try to be poets? Her eyes wandered over the crowd, seeking out Gus Ahern, the owner of Candlewick Inn. She found him leaning up against the side wall just as the auctioneer hammered the bidding into progress.

"One hundred thousand dollars to the gentleman in the front row. One hundred thou; do I hear two?"

The bidding boomeranged back and forth across the room, but Sydney's eyes remained fixed on Gus's long face. His inn...his *home*...going to the highest bidder. Life didn't always treat the Guses of the world fairly, she thought. He should be resting in the cool shade of those trees, not having to uproot himself when roots were nearly all he and Ellie had left.

Gus's lips seemed to react slightly as each bid was topped by the next, but his eyes held a shadowed emptiness. Although she couldn't see too well over the heads of the thick throng of people, Sydney thought she saw a trace of anger there as well.

Out of instinct she wrapped her fingers around the camera that hung from a heavy cord around her neck—then just as quickly let it fall against her thick blue sweater. No, some things were too private, and she surely didn't need a camera to capture the way Gus felt. *She* loved Candlewick, too, and had forever. Some of her earliest memories were woven of sweet-smelling summer days and a young pigtailed girl flying freely across the maple-studded hills that surrounded the stately inn. And when her parents had tired of the trip, she'd come alone and stayed with Grams. And she'd visited Gus and Candlewick Inn and captured in photos what would always be so special to her. She smiled sadly through her thoughts. Yes, it must be almost like letting go of one's child to leave a place you've nurtured so.

"Four hundred thousand dollars! Do I hear five?"

Sydney winced as the microphone shrilled, then shifted her gaze along the other faces lining the far wall. For the first time that afternoon, she noticed the peculiar makeup of the auction crowd. Besides curious neighbors and the serious people from the area whose dream was to buy their own inn, there was a whole new element squeezed into the Candlewick Inn's barn today. Peppered throughout the crowd were professional-looking men in banker's suits and ladies wearing high-heeled shoes and carrying leather brief-cases, looking strangely out of place in the rough-textured room. Everywhere fingers pressed against cheeks and hands lifted quietly and unobtrusively, indicating bids worth more than some of the area people made in a lifetime.

She nudged Lida. "Look at the crowd, Lida. You'd think this was a Sotheby's auction!"

Lida patted her knee gently. "Of course! What did you expect, dear? Have you been in Siberia?"

"Eight hundred thousand dollars," bellowed the auctioneer. *"Do I hear nine? Eight, do I hear nine?"*

Sydney started to pursue Lida's comment, then stopped abruptly as her gaze settled on a tall, lanky man who stood over against the south wall, not far from Gus. His hand lifted noiselessly through the air to the side of his face, and two fingers pressed with practiced finesse to his cheek. Per-haps it was the movement, or maybe his height, that drew her eyes to him, but once he'd caught her attention he held it.

He was the tallest man standing against the wall, his thick, dark hair resting nearly a whole head above the man next to him. The suit and tie were expensively nondescript—bank-er's clothes, Sydney called them—but the ordinariness stopped right there. Even with the cloud of smoke hazing the air between them, Sydney could see the blueness of his eyes. Deep, midnight blue, not clear like the sky, but richer, with a touch of royal purple. They were focused with un-wavering directness on the man at the podium. The even line of his lips were curved slightly, and from Sydney's angle he seemed to be smiling as if playing some whimsical game.

"Eight-five, do I hear nine?"

The tall man's response pleased the auctioneer, who an-nounced the bid and continued his roll.

Sydney couldn't take her eyes off the man. His chin was strong and angled almost roughly, the lines a blend of gentle curve and sharpness. And his fine clothes, worn with ease but not attention, seemed not to matter. They were a convention of society. He was an intriguing blend of contrasts, a photographer's pot of gold. Sydney smiled and breathed deeply.

"Nine hundred thousand, do I hear ten?"

Lida threw Sydney a stern look. "Can't be as good as he looks, dearie—not if he's bidding on Gus's place."

Sydney wrinkled her brow. "Are you prejudiced, Lida? I'll admit, he'd have to change his wardrobe a bit to play innkeeper, but stranger things have happened. The Harrises were from the city, and they run a fine inn over near Green Mountain—"

"Sydney, that's what you get for straddling the fence the way you do, living here, then in the city, then God knows where. Your head's in the sand, dearie—"

"Nine hundred thousand, do we hear nine hundred fifty?..."

"Lida, what are you talking about?"

"Nine hundred fifty thousand to the gentleman. Do I hear nine hundred seventy five?"

"The inn, dearie, the inn!" Lida's sharp voice punctuated the thick, smoky air. "Those slick gentlemen in their funeral suits don't know diddlysquat about inns. They don't want to be innkeepers."

Sydney glanced at the man against the wall. He wasn't leaning any longer but was standing straight now, his eyes still reading, watching, his half smile still in place.

"Nine hundred fifty thousand...going..."

Sydney rubbed her camera, a cold draft creeping into her heart. "What do you mean, Lida?"

"Nine hundred fifty thousand...going..."

"I mean they're going to buy this lovely place, chew it all up and spit it out into the shape of little squat shops where you can buy plastic bottles of syrup and cheap souvenirs and liquor and other things we don't need scarring our hillside, *that's* what I mean, Sydney, dear!"

She folded her arms forcefully over her plump breasts, but it was from Sydney that a rush of air gushed.

"Bulldoze...Candlewick Inn...stores..." Blood pounded in her head as the words registered and Gus's pained white face flashed before her eyes. "Oh, Lida—no—"

Shot with adrenaline, her body surged forward in the chair and one hand flew with the force of a bullet to her flushed face.

And in the time it took for the gavel to pound mightily against the oak table, the crowd's attention focused on Sydney. After counting dramatically into the microphone, the auctioneer puffed out his cheeks victoriously.

"Sold! To the lovely lady in the brilliant blue sweater for nine hundred seventy-five thousand dollars!"

Two

Brian Hennesy spun around and stared at the woman in the blue sweater. She was sitting on the edge of the chair, her eyes wide, her cheeks flushed.

He'd noticed her earlier when she'd come in late. He would have to have been half-blind not to. She had breezed in like a gust of clean air in those formfitting blue jeans, her camera swinging lightly against her breasts, a lovely, self-assured smile on her lips. There'd been something incredibly sensual about that smile, but he'd known he couldn't afford the distraction of exploring it further—even in his mind—before the auction ended. And then a while later he'd caught her looking at *him*, and again he'd had the urge to close the distance between them.

But not once had he seen her bidding. Damn! How had she done it? He was an expert at sniffing out the competition, but he hadn't even considered her.

The crowd around her was buzzing, and the lady next to her was laughing and muttering something to the crowd.

Brian watched carefully; he'd become expert at reading body language as well as lips.

He looked at her eyes. They were extraordinary—large green eyes flecked with gold and brown specks—and wide with embarrassment. Embarrassment...of course! It was a mistake. She hadn't intended to bid at all—a cough, perhaps, or a movement to get up, and the auctioneer had misinterpreted it.

So he *had* gotten the property—or at least the investors and developers he represented had. Brian let the smile ease back across his lips and slowly rotated his shoulders beneath the worsted wool. Good. Another job successfully completed. He could be back to the city by nightfall.

After one last look at the woman in blue, Brian headed for the back door to find the auction officials. They were standing in a clump just outside the inn. He strode over and offered his hand to Jesse Statler, the auction organizer.

"Hello, I'm Brian Hennesy, representing the Goodlin Investment Development Group." His smile broadened. There—nearly all of the searing tension that had spurred him on during the bidding process was gone.

"Yes, Mr. Hennesy, hello." Statler introduced him to the auctioneer, Gus Ahern and a few others. "Seems there's a little confusion here. We...ah...."

"No problem, Mr. Statler, Mr. Ahern," Brian said smoothly. "I've seen it happen before. Sometimes it's difficult to tell an itch from a bid."

Gus Ahern's body was tired and limp, his long face drained of expression. "For a minute I thought Sydney—" He shrugged, shaking his head sadly, then looked up at Brian and nodded. "Well, the bidding was good, Mr. Hennesy, and your offer fair. Guess all that's left is the paperwork."

"Right, Gus." Statler stepped in. "Maybe if we go inside the inn we can talk better, and—"

"Gus, there you are!" the woman in blue cried as she rushed across the cobbled drive.

From the moment she started toward them, Brian's gaze was fixed on her. Her body moved with the graceful ease of a deer, her shoulders lined up just right, her head was held high and the mass of thick shining hair danced to her movements. It moved all at once, he noticed, like a slow-motion ad for shampoo. He breathed deeply, his head filled with a fantasy desire to rush into the ad, sweep her off her feet and ride off on a fine steed with the fair maiden crushed to his chest, her hair blowing in the wind.

Only her voice, rich and filled with laughter, jarred him from his fantasy and stopped him from stepping into the circle and sweeping her away.

"Well, Gus—" Sydney stopped beside the innkeeper and slipped her arm through his "—it seems you and I are to be relatives of a sort!"

Gus's thin lips lifted in a hesitant smile.

Statler's mouth dropped open. "You mean..."

Sydney looked around, her smile bright and steady. "Well, Mr. Statler, I *did* close the auction with my bid, did I not?" She raised her eyebrows in inquiry. "It looks like I'm the new owner of Candlewick Inn!"

Gus's face exploded in a smile. "You mean it, Sydney?"

Brian stepped from the shadows as Gus's sentence circled the group. "Excuse me, Miss—"

Sydney turned toward the voice, and her heart lurched crazily. Whoever this man was, he definitely had a bizarre effect on her basic functions. Her chin lifted and her gaze settled somewhere beneath the thick shock of hair that shadowed his forehead. Up close like this he was even more magnetic, more compelling. Now she could see the sensual set to his jaw, the dark flashes of lightning blue in his eyes. But those things weren't relevant right now, no matter how fast her blood rushed or her pulse beat.

Sydney held out her hand and willed it steady, then marveled at the calmness she feigned. *Sydney, my dear, in the next life, it's the stage for you!* "Hello. I'm Sydney Hanover."

"My competition."

His head tilted slightly to the side when he spoke, his eyes fixed on her face, and Sydney could feel the close scrutiny. It was the kind of look that should have made her uncomfortable, but instead it caused all sorts of other havoc by sending teasing ripples up and down her arms and creating a slight disorientation. She rubbed her arms briskly.

"No, not anymore, we're not." The smile she flashed came easily.

"Oh?"

"The competition is over, Mr—"

"Hennesy. Brian to my friends. Listen, Sydney, we all understand the mistake. It's no problem."

Sydney tipped her head back and smiled headlong into those wonderful eyes. "No, it's no problem at all." And then she tore her eyes from his face and turned her most beguiling smile on Gus Ahern. "That is, it's not a problem if you'll make one tiny concession to the auction rules, Gus...."

"What'll it be, Sydney?" Gus grinned. "Today I feel like I'd lasso the moon for you if you wanted it."

"Give me thirty days to come up with the money."

The small group fell silent.

"That's all I'll need, Gus," Sydney prompted, not wanting the silence to turn against her. Besides, silence meant time to think, and if she had any time to think, it would scare the wits out of her. "Thirty short days, Gus. You and Ellie'll need that much time to pack, anyway—and that way you'll be here for the leaves."

Her cheeks were hot and her heart beat so rapidly now she was sure they could hear it in the next county. *Oh, Sydney, Sydney...* She had gotten herself into unusual predicaments before, but this was the first time she'd come to an auction to pick up an old lamp...and returned home with the deed to an inn!

"Thirty days, you say?" Gus twisted his bony fingers together and half closed his eyes.

"Not the ordinary way to do things, Gus," Statler intoned at his elbow. "You know the Hanovers aren't innkeepers—"

Brian relaxed slightly. So that was it. No real intent at all, just some romantic, spur-of-the-moment notion to buy an inn. And the crazy irony of the whole thing was that waiting awhile would be a boon for his investors. They'd been reluctant to call in their note early—and be penalized—in order to close the deal. A thirty-day delay would be whipped-cream topping on the whole deal. He felt almost guilty about it.

He watched Sydney watch Gus, her eyes bright and hopeful, her breasts moving rhythmically beneath the blue fur of her sweater. He'd heard about women's whims, but this was incredible. A smile played across his lips. Sydney Hanover was an unusual breed.

"Thirty days, Gus, that's all—" Sydney wet her bottom lip. Why was she doing this? Answers escaped her as they often did when emotion swept her away with such force. It must be fate, she'd decided earlier in the barn. She'd honor the bid and then figure out what came next, that was all. It would work out; things always did. And at least Candlewick wouldn't end up a pile of firewood. She breathed deeply and tilted her chin up. "What do you say, Gus?"

Gus seemed to lean into his voice, his small eyes squinting wearily. "I want to, Sydney, sure I do. But what if..."

"If I don't come up with the money?" Sydney looked him directly in the eyes, her voice teasing, and she coaxed a smile to his face. "Then we tell Mr. Hennesy here to pay up and Candlewick is his." Her glance shifted to Brian. He'd been awfully quiet, and Sydney knew she was pushing her luck to outrageous limits. She had no right in the world to suggest he wait like that on an investment. But somehow it didn't matter; if she sounded confident, maybe they'd all think it made sense.

"Just like that?" Brian's thick brows lifted over laughing eyes.

"Just like that."

"Why would I want to wait?"

"Well, there are probably many reasons," Sydney said with assurance.

Gus nodded hopefully.

"You have plenty of other things to occupy your time, I'm sure; it's not like you'd be twiddling your thumbs."

Gus nodded again, while Brian held his silence. Normally he'd be irritated as hell by the brazenness of Sydney Hanover. But he wasn't. He was charmed and delighted, and he found himself wondering what she was doing later that evening. And maybe the next two or three or four. There were more than a few facets to Sydney he'd love to explore further. "Go on."

"And I can tell by that look in your eyes, Mr. Hennesy, that you don't for one half second doubt that I'll fail in getting the money. So you have nothing to lose." She paused, palms balanced on her hips, her head held back so he could see the intriguing challenge lighting her eyes. "And there's another thing—"

This time it was Brian who nodded, a glimmer of fun lighting his eyes.

"You look like a man who likes a challenge." Her flashing hazel eyes locked with his. "So I daresay you'll agree to this simply to prove you can win. If you refuse me a chance and take the inn now, there's no challenge in it, is there?"

"Nope. No challenge at all."

"So. Then it's a deal?" She turned to Gus before Brian had a chance to reply. "See, Gus, you can't lose. Winner takes all, but you're assured of at least one winner."

Gus pumped her hand. "It's a deal, Sydney: thirty days, provided Mr. Hennesy here agrees. And we'll postpone the furnishings auction until all this is decided." He hugged her then—a bony, thin hug that left a warm, deep feeling in its wake.

Sydney hugged him back. "Mr. Hennesy agrees." She sneaked a look over Gus's shoulder at Brian Hennesy and tried to read the look on his face. Challenge? Amusement? One thing was clear: he was taking her about as seriously as a mosquito bite. But that was just fine. He might not take her seriously now, but there was no way in hell he was going to get his hands on Candlewick Inn. She smiled sweetly and pulled herself away from Gus.

"Well, Gus," Mr. Statler said over Sydney's head, "Guess we'd better go inside and look over those papers, see what we need to do next."

Gus smiled broadly. "Guess we'd better."

The two walked off with the auctioneer in tow and Sydney turned back to Brian Hennesy. "Well, thank you, Mr. Hennesy, for being so gracious about this."

"No problem. I'm a gracious human being." His eyes seemed to bore right down deep inside her, but Sydney didn't back off.

She met his look straight on, even though she knew it was turning dangerous. "So I guess the thirty-days war has begun...."

Brian reached out and took her hand. "I suppose this needs at least a handshake."

"To seal it—"

"At the least—" His hand swallowed hers, then let it slip away. Before Sydney had a chance to react, his arm wrapped around her and he pulled her close. "Actually, a handshake won't quite do it. We're talking major agreement here. After all, I may lose my job over this."

Sydney looked up, but he was so close she could barely see him. "Your job?" she murmured softly into the delicious medley of sensations floating around her. His dark head was backlighted by the sun, but she could see the half smile, sensuous and tempting, as he nodded.

"But a deal's a deal once it's sealed," Brian said, lowering his head to close the remaining inch of space between them. He kissed her gently and carefully but without any trace of shyness. He had anticipated the sweetness, the warmth, but not the surge of desire that shot through him as he held her close.

Sydney reacted instinctively, a response born in pure and simple emotion. Her lips parted and her whole body filled with a delicious flow of sweet passion. She would quite possibly have sustained the kiss for some time if she hadn't felt her breath being cut off and a sharp stab of pain piercing her breasts. With considerable effort she wound her fingers around his upper arms and pushed him away.

"The camera," she murmured, drawing his eyes down to the hanging Minolta that had been wedged sharply between them.

Brian stared at it. He hadn't felt a thing. In that one brief kiss, the lovely softness of Sydney Hanover had effectively taken over his body and soul. His eyes lifted to hers. "Sorry. I forgot about the camera."

The rush of cool air settled Sydney's heartbeat somewhat. "I don't think it nullified the deal any—"

"No, I'm sure not. I think it's pretty well sealed."

"Yes, sealed tightly."

"With dynamite. Thirty days, then?"

"Thirty days." Sydney backed away, her hands returning to the cool comfort of her camera but her eyes lingering in the pools of midnight-blue darkness. "You can leave the information with Gus. You know, your phone number, etcetera."

Brian didn't say a word. He slipped his hands into the pockets of his trousers and watched her lean body move backward across the drive. He had felt the loveliness of those curves when he held her close, and now he could see their beauty from a distance. And the vibrancy that spilled from her eyes was the same that had tingled beneath his fingers and pressed into his lips as he'd kissed her. He wondered how he could stop it all, freeze it and save it for himself.

"We'll be in touch." Her voice floated across the drive to where he stood, and Brian managed a lopsided grin.

"You can bet on that."

"Enough gambles for one day, Mr. Hennesy," she called as she slipped into a small red Volkswagen and gunned the engine.

Anything she might have added was lost beneath the spitting sound of gravel as the car spun into a turn and disappeared down the long, wooded driveway.

Brian stood there for a long time, his hands in his pockets, his eyes following the tire marks in the driveway. They were proof she'd been there, proof he hadn't imagined the fiery woman with the camera around her neck. And he'd made a deal with her.

A satisfied smile began to play across his face. Not only would the Goodlin Group be pleased, but with the intuition that had propelled him to the top of the financial field, he knew without question it was going to be the most interesting autumn of his busy career.

With a wave to the deserted driveway and the absent woman who had lighted an autumn bonfire beneath his three-piece suit, Brian Hennesy turned slowly and walked to the Candlewick Inn.

Three

Sydney sat at the bay window of her grandmother's spacious house and looked out toward the soothing green fields that rolled off into the dusk. Her thoughts were muddled. Candlewick Inn—that was what she needed to be thinking about. The inn and a slight matter of nearly one million dollars. But images of the tall man with the midnight-blue eyes kept scattering her orderly thoughts into fuzzy wisps that she couldn't hang on to.

She tapped on the pane absentmindedly with the tip of a pencil. Three robins, their red chests puffed lifted gracefully from a gnarled limb rubbing the window. Regarding Sydney coolly, they glided off to quieter quarters.

"Concentrate, Sydney," she whispered aloud, and reached for a square pad of paper on the kitchen counter. One million dollars. That wasn't totally impossible.... She'd simply have to plan a little. No, she'd have to plan a lot.

Her pencil played a staccato rhythm on the round oak table. It was worth it. Once the inn was safe from those lecherous investment monsters, she could leisurely find another buyer who was interested in the inn, or she could hire someone to run it. Or she could...well, there were probably other options, as well. They would come to her eventually. One thing at a time.

The blank pad at her fingertips filled with invisible thoughts. Was it just yesterday she was congratulating herself on the order she'd managed to tuck into her life? Her friendly three-year engagement to Stanley Woolfe was over. Ended. And she knew Stan felt the lifting of an enormous, suffocating weight from his spirit nearly as acutely as she did. That kind of commitment didn't suit either of them, and the overdue parting was a release of such proportions that it surprised Sydney. Perhaps she was more like her mother than she dared admit.

And then *Vermont Today* had stepped in and commissioned her to take six months' worth of photographs; that was six months of lovely, leisurely work, which would give her plenty of time to clean out all the remaining cobwebs and move ahead with her life.

And today, in a fraction of a second, it had all been shot to blazes.

"Sydney, dear," a worn, amused voice said, interrupting her thoughts, "you're putting ruts in my table with your pencil."

Sydney looked up quickly. "Grams, you startled me."

A small, elderly lady with pure white hair eased her bent body into a chair beside her granddaughter. "A million dollars for your thoughts, darling."

Sydney moaned. "Lida called."

"Certainly." She nodded her diminutive head calmly, but her clear blue eyes jumped with excitement. "Seems you're buying Candlewick Inn. It makes me wonder what you would have purchased, dearie, if I had sent you to the auction to buy something bigger than my lamp."

"And I didn't even manage to get the lamp!" Sydney laughed. "What do you think, Grams? Have I bitten off too big a chunk this time?"

"It's more like a mountain, I'd say."

"Do you think I'm crazy?"

Grams reached over and patted Sydney's hand. "I think it's all in the genes, Sydney Elizabeth Spencer Hanover. I don't see as how you've much control over it."

The glint in Grams's eyes brought a quick smile to Sydney's face. "And whose genes are we talking about here?"

"The Spencers', of course. My papa would have done the same thing. And if I weren't so tired—" She shook her head slowly and tiny sprigs of white fluff glistened in the fading sunlight.

"So you're to blame for this impulsive streak that gets me in hot water—"

"To blame or to credit?" Gram's tired eyes were bright. "Your life is certainly a good sight more interesting than some of the Hanovers'." Gram patted Sydney's cheek. "Yes, Sydney, I shall take all the credit for this."

"Fine, Grams, then you'll help me come up with a million dollars in thirty days?"

Hortense Spencer's delicate brows drew together in thought and her eyes grew hazy with a faraway look. "I could, you know. If only I could remember—"

Sydney wrapped one arm around Grams's thin shoulders. Aging had sped up its course on Grams this year, and it troubled Sydney, especially at times like this when Grams was so vibrant one minute, so lost in memory the next. "Don't you worry your beautiful head about it, Grams. I'll give it that valiant Spencer try."

"Of course you will, my sweet wildflower, of course you will." She sat up a little straighter and pushed a stray white hair into place, the light brightening in her eyes again. "Now, let's plot a little strategy here, and analyze the enemy—"

"Grams, I think cable TV will be the ruin of you!"

Gram tittered softly and poured two glasses of sherry from a delicate crystal container that sat in the middle of the table. "We'll see, sweetie. Now tell me about him."

"Who?"

"The tall, good-looking gentleman who jarred Lida's pacemaker, of course. The enemy. We need to examine his weak spots."

Enemy... Brian Hennesy didn't fit the word exactly, although Sydney supposed the title was appropriate. But certainly enemies didn't kiss like that. And she was sure Brian Hennesy had *no* weak spots. She hadn't felt any, anyway, when his well-muscled body had pressed against her own.

The gentle tinkling of the wind chimes Grams used as a doorbell cooled the heat that was creeping uncomfortably up Sydney's neck.

Grams looked toward the door, one thin brow raised. Her neighbors didn't often bother with the chimes, but simply walked in through the unlocked door and made themselves comfortable in the lovely home that always smelled of lilacs. She took a quick sip of sherry. "Curses. Just as we were drawing up the battle plan."

"It'll wait, Grams. I'll get the door."

Sydney left the cheery country kitchen and walked through the wide hallway that led to the front of the house. From every room late afternoon sunshine poured in on the white-pine floors and family heirloom furniture. Sydney loved it here, loved the tradition and the clean beauty and the honesty of the old woman who was as close to her heart as her own parents were. Perhaps closer in some ways. The chimes tinkled again, more insistently this time, and she quickly opened the carved mahogany door.

He still had his suit on, but the tie was gone and the crisp cotton shirt was pulled apart just enough to reveal the shadow of dark chest hair. And his smile was in place—slightly lopsided, but with a proper and businesslike edge. It was the eyes that brought back the heat of his kiss, and

Sydney felt a strange melting sensation just behind her knees. "Oh. Hello," she managed huskily.

"Oh, hello, to you, too. I hope I'm not interrupting anything—"

"Who is it, Sydney, dear?" Grams's voice drifted in from the kitchen.

"The enemy, Grams," Sydney murmured.

Brian lifted one brow, his head leaning to one side and his midnight-blue eyes never leaving Sydney's face.

"Oh, gracious goodness! Bring him in, dear."

"Come, Mr. Hennesy," Sydney said with a small smile. "Come meet my grandmother."

Brian followed her silently through the hallway, his mind formulating an excuse for showing up on her doorstep. The papers had all been checked and everything was in proper order. He'd have the inn in thirty days, as soon as Sydney defaulted on her deadline; and thanks to Sydney's impulsiveness, his clients would save a lot of money in the long run. So why was he here instead of stretched out on the wide four-poster in that airy room over at the inn? The answer his body gave him wasn't enough. Sure, he wanted her. She was as sensuous a woman as he'd ever seen. Sensuous and sensual, but definitely not the kind of woman you loved and left.

Which left him back at zero in the explanations department, an oddly unfamiliar place for Brian Hennesy to be.

"Grams," Sydney was saying as she stood silhouetted against the fading light from the windows, "this is Mr. Brian Hennesy, the other bidder on the inn. Brian, my grandmother, Hortense Spencer."

Grams was silent for a moment as she allowed Brian to shake her bony hand and wrap her in a charming smile, and Sydney could see she was sizing him up. "Mr. Hennesy," she said after a moment, "please sit. Sydney and I were just talking about you."

Brian's smile didn't change, but he seemed to Sydney to be digesting the information and enjoying it.

"Talking about Candlewick Inn, Grams means. And the deal we've made."

Brian nodded solemnly. "I see. And what do you think of it, Mrs. Spencer?"

"Oh, Mr. Hennesy, what I think isn't worth a tinker's damn, don't you see? It's what Sydney thinks. And she thinks she's going to own the inn in thirty days." Grams's mouth drew up into a pleased smile.

"Oh, she does, does she?" Brian lifted one thick brow and looked over at Sydney, who was watching him closely.

"Does that surprise you?" Sydney asked. "I certainly wouldn't take something like this on if I wasn't determined to wi—to achieve my goal."

Brian's eyes were laughing openly now. "You almost said win, didn't you? You do see this as a contest." The thought amused him at first and then delighted him. Having a contest with Sydney Hanover carried with it a whole set of connotations he wasn't at all reluctant to explore.

Sydney ignored his comment and looked at him carefully, trying to figure out what it was about him that was making her anxious. It was something important, she knew. Something important to her life. A connection taking place at a time when she wasn't in the market for connections. "Why are you here, Mr. Hennesy? Is there some unfinished business we need to take care of?"

"Why am I here? Well, since I am more or less going to be sticking around this little town for a month, and since you are one of the few people I know here, *and* since this situation exists because of you, I thought perhaps you would show me around. Would you?"

"Was that mouthful carefully thought out?"

"Actually, no." Brian smiled openly. "It all came to me in a flash as my mouth opened. But it makes perfect sense to me. What do you think, Hortense?"

Sydney saw them joining forces, her grandmother and the man who just hours ago was a stranger. She wasn't sure what they were rallying for or against, but at that precise moment she felt defenseless, naked, somehow. Grams didn't give her a chance to speak.

"As a matter of fact, Brian, I think that's a wonderful idea. Certainly fair. Sydney *will* get the inn when all is said and done, but there isn't any reason we can't deal with it all in a cheery and pleasant manner." She took another sip of sherry. "I believe I will retire there—in the inn, I mean. I'm eighty-seven, you know."

Grams's frail body leaned over the table toward Brian. Her small white head bent slightly in a conspiratorial way. "I would invite you to dinner, Brian, but the pickings are slim. Perhaps Sydney will take you to dinner in town and see that you find your way about." Her thin brows lifted when she looked at Sydney, and Sydney could see the delight in the crinkly blue eyes.

She shook her head, smiling at Hortense Spencer's maneuvers. "Sure, Grams, that makes sense. You come with us."

Grams held her head between her bony fingers and feigned a look of complete exhaustion. "No, Sydney, darling. I have a bowl of soup on the stove and my music to lull me to sleep. My bones are weary tonight. Off with you two." She swept the air with her hand as she might have done chasing off a mosquito, then pushed herself up from the chair. "I need my sleep, you know." With a sweet smile that Sydney found vaguely inappropriate, she shuffled from the room.

"I've put you on the spot." Brian lifted one of the sherry glasses and examined the intricate cut-crystal design. His voice held no remorse.

"Yes, you did. But you're right. You were gracious to agree to the terms, and the least I can do is show you around." She rose from her chair and smiled brightly. "That should take all of five minutes. Greenbriar isn't very large, as you must have noticed."

Yes, Brian had noticed, he assured her as they walked out into the crisp New England dusk. He wasn't quite sure how he felt about it, either.

"You're a big-city person?"

He nodded. "But I end up in small towns like this now and then on business. However, I manage never to stay long enough to realize the smallness."

"Afraid it will eat you?" Sydney laughed. He didn't answer but laughed along with her, and when she looked at him sideways she saw the lines that edged his eyes when he smiled. They were nice lines, she thought, and she found herself wondering about the events and years that defined them. "Well, Greenbriar won't eat you, I promise. The people here are basic, honest folks who accept you as you are, as long as you don't scare the cows or disturb their lives in any significant way."

They had reached the end of Grams's driveway and were heading along a narrow, tree-lined path that led into town. Brian had removed his suit coat, and it hung lazily over one shoulder, swinging lightly as they walked. Sydney fell into the rhythm of his long steps and enjoyed the slight breeze his body made as it moved beside her, occasionally brushing pleasantly against her shoulder.

Brian looked over at her thoughtfully, her words repeating in his mind. "But I have disturbed their lives, I suppose."

"No, you haven't. You almost did, but not quite."

"I see." *Almost did.* The contest again. The war of the inn. "Sydney, you're an unusual woman."

Sydney frowned. "Unusual? That could mean all sorts of things." She tossed her head. "And I don't think I'm up to any of them on an empty stomach. I suggest we head for Widow Mathews's Tavern. She serves ham steaks she smokes herself and buttermilk biscuits that you'll die for. After that you can have your tour."

Brian found himself quite willing to settle for that, as long as she was there beside him and the fresh smell of her continued to waft around him like a magical cloud. He sat down at the checker-clothed table in the tavern and took in the homey, rustic surroundings before resting his gaze once more on Sydney's face. "I want to know more about you, Sydney Hanover."

Sydney was silent for a moment, then cupped her chin in her hands and asked honestly, "Why?"

"I've never met anyone like you."

"Probably not, Brian. If your profession is any indication of your life, the circles we run in are quite different."

He couldn't tell if there was criticism in her voice, or if it was merely an honest statement. "I take it you don't think much of my profession."

"I'm not even sure what it is."

"Maybe if I told you, we could forget about it."

"Try me," she said.

"I'm a business consultant. People who want to make money investing and developing land hire me to check it out, make suggestions, pull the necessary money together and make the best deal."

"And do you?"

"Always."

"And then you walk away with a chunk of the profits."

Laughter spilled from his eyes. "Are you trying to check me out, Ms. Hanover?"

She lifted one shoulder in a playful shrug. "Sure, why not? It can't hurt to know what I'm up against."

A pretty waitress in a yellow plaid apron interrupted them with a recitation of the day's specials. She grinned at Sydney. "But I know you, Sydney, it's the Widow's ham and biscuits and apple pie. Right?"

"Right, Frances. And let's give my friend the same so he'll see what he's missing by living in the city."

Brian's head lifted with a start. People rarely made decisions for him, even about trivial things like menu items. He waited for the irritation to come. But none came, and the only emotion he felt was the same gentle wave of intrigue and delight that had played around him for hours now. He smiled and shook his head. Hell, she was a witch. It was the only possible explanation. Either that or he was so far overdue for a rest that his mind had given up and folded in on itself. In which case he wasn't responsible for his actions, so maybe his best bet was to go with the flow.

The waitress nodded and hurried off, her brown ponytail sashaying between her shoulder bones. Brian watched her walk away, then looked at Sydney. He leaned forward slightly, his forearms resting on the tablecloth. "Is this your home, Sydney?"

"Sometimes."

"And other times?"

"Here and there. I spent a lot of time here with Grams when I was little, and I keep coming back. More often recently, it seems."

"Is there a reason for that?"

"Yes. Several actually. The one you would understand best is that I have a job here. A magazine has commissioned me to do a series of area photographs for them."

Brian nodded, understanding, yet slightly irritated that she pegged him so rigidly. Business wasn't his whole life, after all. Even though he'd be hard-pressed to prove it in recent years.

"And you live with your grandmother when you're here, according to the people at the inn."

"Yes. We're very close."

Brian listened carefully. That fit in with what he had seen in the peaceful home on the edge of town. Maneuvering cold business deals for years had at least granted Brian that trait: he tuned in quickly to the signals people sent one another and to the vibrations that passed between them. He sensed things immediately and usually quite accurately. And he had made a lot of money because he used his knowledge as a lever to work out the best deals. That thought seemed so out of place at the small, rough table in the dark, good-smelling tavern in this New England hamlet that Brian nearly

laughed. But he held it back and focused again on Sydney.
"And your grandmother wants to move to the inn?"

"Oh, I first heard about that when you did. We haven't
really had a lot of time to plan. But the inn *is* very special to
Grams, just as it is to many people around here."

She was putting it between them, the "deal," and Brian
wished it could be forgotten for tonight. But it couldn't, so
at least he could try to understand. "Special? How so?"

"Oh, everyone has his or her own reasons, I suppose. But
for Grams it was where she spent her wedding night. And in
one of those big, airy rooms with the moon hanging low and
the smell of the honey drifting in, she claims my mother was
given life."

Sydney leaned back in her chair as the waitress set down
a heavy plate heaped with thick slices of ham and potatoes.
In the center of the table she placed a woven basket of biscuits so hot that curls of steam slipped through the napkin
folds and warmed the air between them. Sydney saw Brian's
delighted, hungry look and laughed. "Aha, behind that
designer suit lurks a bit of country."

"Could be." He beamed at Sydney and lifted his fork.
"Or it could simply be starvation. I didn't realize until this
minute that I haven't eaten all day. This looks great."

Sydney watched him as he devoured the spicy meat and
drank his hot coffee. She pushed her food around her plate,
feeling again the connection and the surprising comfort of
sitting across the cluttered table from Brian Hennesy, enemy. He wasn't even looking at her now, but the tension was
there, stretched as tight as a fiddle's strings. She shifted in
the chair and tried to figure out the day and the predica-
ment and the curious twist of fate that had put her here.
Through a haze of food smells and tavern smoke, she
watched him and smiled as the contented sheen of a well-fed
man began to spread across his face.

"Hey, you're not eating." Brian eyed her plate, and she
gently pushed it through the maze of salt and pepper shak-
ers and butter plates.

Brian grinned. "Thanks. Don't mind if I do." And he polished off her half-eaten ham steak until the plate was shiny and clean. "Fantastic. You may have to roll me out of here, Sydney, but it will be well worth it."

Over apple pie he told her how tired he was eating hotel food, that the Widow's Tavern was a bit of heaven in a long line of fancy, rich-sauced entrecotes. He contorted his face as he exaggerated the pronunciation, and Sydney's laughter floated over and met his.

"I need that tour now, or I won't fit into the one and only suit I brought with me."

Sydney worked at keeping her eyes from exploring the truth of his statement. "Tour it is, then."

Brian pulled out a plastic card to pay for their dinners, left a generous tip beneath the empty roll basket and guided Sydney out into the darkening night.

The lampposts dotting the main street of Greenbriar cast a hazy glow across the town. Store lights flickered on, and strollers created long shadows across the curbs.

"You know, this would be far more effective in the morning when you could see things," Sydney suggested.

Brian slipped an arm over her shoulder and said, "I like seeing things through the lamplight. Where's our sense of romantic adventure?" His fingers on her shoulder rubbed lightly against the blue fur of her sweater.

Brian's familiarity was causing heat beneath the soft yarn, and Sydney wondered briefly if he could feel it. Then he'd know where *her* sense of romantic adventure was at that moment. She took a deep breath and shut her eyes briefly. When she opened them, her mind was functioning more clearly. "This is business, remember?"

Brian grinned down at her, but his eyes held mischief. "Whatever you say."

"This is a simple courtesy since you'll be staying here for a—" She stopped beneath a lamp and looked at him sideways, her mind going in different directions to block out the heat of his touch. "Why *are* you staying here? Why aren't

you going back to your office or working on some new
deals?'' As the words came out, she realized that they were
legitimate. Why *was* he sticking around? The lawyer had
said his offices were in New York, and it was only a few
hours away. There was no reason for him to hang around,
unless— ''Of course! That's it; how dumb of me!'' Her
palm came up and slapped her forehead.

Brian looked at her with amusement. ''Sydney, you lost
me a while back.''

''You're staying around here to check on me. To keep an
eye on me.'' She shook loose from his light caress and stood
apart, staring at him.

''You could hardly blame me for that. You're a beautiful
woman,'' he said quietly.

''No, Brian, it's this business deal. That's why you're
hanging around—to protect your interests, to find out my
plans. But you don't really need to go through such subter-
fuge, you know. My strategy is simple and straightfor-
ward.'' Her words were coming out pell-mell now, like
bullets from a Gatling gun, and she couldn't stop. ''I'm
going to get people to either invest in the inn, or to loan me
the money. And then I will buy it. Fair and square.''

Brian struggled with the sensations passing swiftly
through him. They had nothing to do with anger or business contracts or investors. The flashing gold in her wide
eyes and the huskiness in her voice, swelled now with emotion, the rise and fall of her breasts, were creating havoc in
a very basic, age-old manner. Brian Hennesy was aroused.

He shifted uncomfortably. He wanted to lay a hand on
her shoulder to calm her down and assure her he was not
spying on her, but he was afraid to touch her.

''Well?'' Sydney stared arrows into him. ''Aren't you
going to at least show some feeble form of repentance?''

But as she looked challengingly into his unreadable eyes,
Sydney began to calm down, realizing almost immediately
that she was overreacting. A Spencer trait, Grams had told
her often, one her mother had inherited full force, but which

she, Sydney, seemed to have gotten only a small dab of, thank heavens. And it only burst out when she felt out of control of a situation. As she did now.

"I apologize." Brian smiled softly. "Maybe there was a little of that mixed up in my motivations. It's instinct, and you'll have to pardon it." But he knew as he spoke it was only the tiniest part of his motivations. "Am I forgiven?"

Sydney looked into the midnight-blue eyes and saw the gentle laughter held there. She wanted to keep looking, to let the deep blue sea swallow her. She wanted to take a picture of just his eyes and forehead, with the smallest hint of a thick wave of dark brown hair falling carelessly above, and she wanted to keep it framed in her mind. "Forgiven?"

"Yes." He lifted a wave of coppery hair and let it slide through his fingers. "For wanting to spy on you."

The meaning of his words was muted by the tension that flowed between them until he might as well have kept silent. They were like lovers' words that didn't need to make sense but were carried on a deeper crest of meaning that gave them life. Sydney nodded slowly.

"Good," Brian said.

"The tour...?"

Brian tore his eyes away and looked down the winding street. "I guess we ought to proceed."

"I think that's a good idea." Sydney noticed that the evening light was clearing, becoming more focused, and the mottled colors she'd seen seconds ago were sharpening into the cool gray of the sidewalk and the deep green of the grassy finger of earth along the curb. When she shook her head, the picture she'd taken in her mind faded. "I think it will be the ten-cents tour, Brian. I'm suddenly very tired."

She started walking down the street, but Brian caught her by the arm and turned her back to him.

"Brian...?"

He was watching her with a half smile, and his dark eyes pierced through her like a sword. "I think maybe the tour should wait, Sydney. And what I really want, which is to

take you back to my room at the inn, will have to wait, too,
I know." His hands smoothed up and down her arms while
he talked. "But it's a little difficult for me to pay attention
to landmarks and objects of town pride under these condi-
tions. So I'm going to do the honorable thing and take you
home."

Sydney nodded. She'd never been accused of being short
on words, but then she'd never before met anyone like Brian
Hennesy.

Without further ceremony he took her arm and they
walked back to the old-fashioned gate leading up to Grams's
house.

The warmth of her body was not something Brian wanted
to let go of. For a moment he just looked at her.

"I think I'll go in," she said slowly. She touched his cheek
briefly.

Tenderness lighted Brian's eyes. "This is all a little complicated, isn't it?" Before she could answer, he dipped his
head briefly, brushed a kiss across her lips and left.

Sydney turned when she reached the doorway. She could
still see him, his figure faint against the moonlight, walking
toward town. She sighed, wondering if she should start
reading her horoscope in the newspaper, then quickly dis-
carded the idea.

The *Greenbriar Gazette* wouldn't be able to handle the
mail if they accurately predicted the kind of day she'd just
had.

Four

Sydney breezed into the inn's lobby and smiled at the man behind the curved reception desk. "Hi, handsome. You're looking very chipper this afternoon."

"Well, my dear Sydney, I have you to thank for that." Gus leaned his bony elbows down on the knotty pine and beckoned Sydney close. "Ellie and I have a whole new lease on life because of you, young lady."

Sydney fingered her camera nervously. "Now, Gus, you know I'm going to try my best, and I have every reason to believe I can pull this off, but there is that tiny outside chance that—"

"Shush, now, Sydney. Talking like that'll bring you nothing but failure. You're going to get that money, and Candlewick Inn is going to stay on the map. That's that!"

Sydney didn't answer. Instead she walked over and poured herself a cup of coffee from the large silver urn on the corner table. Gus was right. It was simply the intensity of the project that was making her edgy, and letting it sit for

a day should ease that some. Slowly she stirred in a generous portion of cream, and by the time the amorphous bands
of color had blended together, her assurance had returned.

When she looked up, Gus's long face was thoughtful.
"You know, Sydney, leaving the inn is a decision Ellie and
I knew was inevitable. She can't take the winters anymore,
and the thought of her relaxing and soaking up sunshine in
Arizona is a grand thing. And we can come back here in
summers and falls whenever we want. That's all good. But
what's *bad*—and rotten and painful to boot—is the thought
of Candlewick Inn disappearing from the face of the earth.
That's what turns our insides to sour milk."

Sydney nodded. "I know, Gus. I don't understand how
anyone could even think about doing that, business deal or
not." She looked around at the comforting pine walls of the
inn and felt a sweet wash of memory. This place had been a
second home to her for as long as she could remember, an
annex to Grams's house that always welcomed her. Everything remained comfortingly the same at Candlewick Inn—
the homey smells, the worn, braided rugs on the floor, the
soft light that played across the solid tables, oversize chairs
and colorful cushions of the couches—and it had brought
an order to the chaotic life she lived with her mother. The
young Sydney had desperately needed that order. A week in
Greenbriar, or a month or a summer, always put her back
together and returned her to her mother or her father re-
vived and ready to cope. And now the older Sydney found
the same need, the same magical haven in Greenbriar and
the Candlewick Inn.

She looked up and saw Gus watching her, his face mir-
roring her feelings. Of course it did; he had even more in-
vested here than she did. She nodded, and the unspoken
emotion settled tenderly between them.

"So, Sydney," Gus said at last, breaking the moment by
busying himself with a stack of reservations, "what brings
you over here this morning? The grapevine tells me you've
been holed up burning phone wires from dawn till mid-

night these past few days. Working out deals and things, I suppose." His gray brows lifted expectantly.

"Yes. And I'm making progress. But today I'm back to taking pictures for a little while. It keeps me balanced."

"Hortense told me you're taking some pictures for *Vermont Today*. Good for you, young lady!"

"Thanks, Gus." Sydney flashed him a proud smile. "The light is so perfect this afternoon, I thought I'd hike out to Candlewick Pond and see what I can find."

"Good idea. Get some clean air in those lungs to keep you going. By the way, Sydney—" Gus paused until Sydney turned toward him and he had her full attention. "Looks like that Mr. Hennesy hasn't let any grass grow under his feet, either. He's been making plenty of phone calls this week, too."

Sydney put her fists on her hips and frowned. "Gus! You're not—"

Gus shook his head vehemently, and thin gray hairs caught and waved in the breeze. "No, sirree, I don't eavesdrop. Just loggin' my charts here. We keep track of long-distance calls, you know."

"Oh," Sydney said. She kept her eyes cool, disinterested, just a trifle curious. "So... he's been here since the auction?" She hadn't heard a word from or about Brian Hennesy in four days—not since he'd walked her back to Grams's on Saturday night. There'd been no request for another tour, no bumping into him at the post office or gas station. Nothing. It was a blessing, she'd told herself. Don't fraternize with the enemy. Don't become muddled in your thinking. Don't... don't... don't... But the blessings and don'ts left her feeling strangely empty inside.

"Well, he's been here and not been here. Busy man, that Mr. Hennesy. He made a bunch of phone calls, as I told you, then filled up the gas tank and drove to New York. Showed up at bedtime that day with two suitcases. Clothes, don't you see? That and phone calls about does it."

"How did you know I was in New York?" The deep voice sounded just behind Sydney, so close she could feel the words curve across the thin back of her T-shirt. She turned slowly. Although he was speaking to Gus, his eyes were on her, and his free hand lifted and settled with natural ease on her shoulder. In his other arm he held two shopping bags with names of local stores in script across the shiny paper.

"Well, hello, Mr. Hennesy," Gus said with only a slight touch of embarrassment. He considered keeping track of his guests a form of compliment. More than once he and his dog Mo had taken to the trail to rescue a lost hiker in the woods. "It's plain and simple how I knew. Harry Friedman owns the gas station and has breakfast here every morning. It takes one fill up and about as many hours as you disappeared to go to New York and back. Montpelier'd only take a third as much; besides, you left from the other side of town."

Brian laughed. "Gus, if ever I need a private eye—"

"At your service," the old man said.

They were awfully friendly, Sydney thought, for two men who looked at life so differently and were sitting on opposite sides of the fence. Brian seemed to have charmed Gus into being his friend, even as he was waiting out the time until the inn could be torn apart. It didn't make sense. Yet hadn't he almost done the same thing to her? Made her feel nice and warm and attracted to him?

Suddenly it all seemed like a giant ploy. Tactics. Maneuvers. The thought made her stiffen, and Brian felt the slight shift beneath his fingers.

"Want to see my loot?" he asked quietly.

No, she didn't want to see his loot. And she'd be better off not seeing him. She owed it to Gus to keep her mind clear, her vision in front of her. She'd seen enough, and it was a distraction she simply couldn't afford right now.

"Good," Brian said, and lowered the bags to the floor. He dipped into one and pulled out a pair of binoculars.

So, Sydney thought, now he can spy with assistance.

"I don't know a cardinal from a meadowlark," Brian was saying, his voice holding a hint of boyish excitement that seemed strangely incongruous to Sydney. "Now's the time to put it straight." The next item out of his sack was a navy-blue backpack with so many zippers on the front, Sydney suspected it reversed into a straitjacket if needed.

"To wander in yonder woods," he explained, looking out the back windows into the rising stretch of wooded foothills.

Sydney listened carefully. His voice was deep and had a touch of devastating gentleness that steadily worked away at her reserve.

The backpack was followed by a jacket that folded into a pouch, a thermos jug and a Swiss Army knife still in the box. "And last but not least—" Brian spread the folds of the second bag and pulled out a small maple-framed photo of a mountain lake. Dusk hung over the deep water in heavy folds, and the photographer had managed to catch the day's last streaks of sunlight just as they penetrated the mist. "To adorn my temporary quarters—"

Sydney took a quick breath. "Brian, what—?"

His smile showed how pleased he was with his purchase. "You're very good, Sydney. The lady in the gift shop says she can't keep your photographs in stock. The locals love them and all the 'city folk' want them in their cabins. She included me in that last group, so I bought one. I didn't know you were a celebrity around here."

Sydney shrugged but didn't try to mask the pleasure she felt. It seemed such a personal gesture, somehow, his buying one of her photos. Brian showed the photo to Gus, then carefully wrapped it in the tissue.

Sydney stood quietly watching his purposeful movements, his strong blunt fingers pressing thin pieces of tissue in place. From her position above him, she couldn't see all of his face, just the angular profile and his body bent in strong lines and curves.

The suit was gone. Today he was wearing khaki slacks with a dark blue knit shirt that was stretched across an expanse of chest less noteworthy for its broadness than for the firm mould of muscles just visible beneath the fine material. Casual expense, the clothes said, but Brian was no different in them than he'd been in a finely tailored suit. And Sydney suspected clothes mattered little to him. She quickly pulled her eyes away and concentrated on the newly purchased thermos he had handed up to her.

"You're not very talkative, Sydney." He was still on his knees, but his head tilted back and he looked at her carefully. "Anything wrong?"

She rolled the smooth, cool thermos back and forth between her palms, then paused and looked at it seriously. "Nope. I'm just admiring this thermos. It's a great picture of Mr. T." She twisted the blue cylinder around and pointed at the massive man staring out from the plastic. Her face softened into a grin. "He's cute. An idol?"

Brian laughed. "I guess I was in a hurry." He took it from her and slipped it into the bag.

"Looks like you're planning some heavy camping, Brian," Gus joked.

"Well, Gus, I figure it's a start." Brian stretched his long body up to full height, and forked his fingers through thick, dark hair. "When you consider the roughest going I've had in fifteen years has been a broken toilet at the Waldorf in Chicago, well, you can see I've got to take things one step at a time."

"I know an easy way to start, then." Gus's bony hand slapped down on the desk as if he'd just invented electricity. "You go on out with Sydney this afternoon. She knows this area like the back of her pretty hand, and she'll introduce you to the wilds nice and slow."

"Gus—" Sydney frowned, then looked at Brian. "No offense, Brian, but I'm going to be working."

Brian eyed the camera. "I could carry your flashbulbs."

"I don't use flashbulbs."

"Film? Surely you use film."

His crooked smile entered her senses with a rush. She tried to hit him with her I-mean-business look, but it turned into a laughing shrug and failed completely. "Oh, sure—come along. But you're going to have to keep quiet when I say so. I can't have you scaring off my subjects."

"It's the farthest thing from my mind. Honest."

She looked at him sideways. "You may be bored, you know."

"Not a chance in two lifetimes of that." And before she could ponder any longer, he scooped up his bags, deposited them behind Gus's desk for safekeeping and encouraged her out the back door, a brand-new navy-blue backpack swinging lightly from one shoulder.

There was nothing predictable about Brian Hennesy, Sydney decided as they walked single file through a narrow path in the thick woods that filled the northern section of the inn's property. She thought of a photo study she'd done a year ago of successful men-about-town. The study had been commissioned by a slick city magazine that put its money into the quality of paper rather than a full-time staff.

She'd pulled six men out of the list of suggestions. Then she'd spent a sunny July week photographing them working, attending meetings, lunching at chic, several-martini restaurants and walking down the avenue with their three-piece suits wrinkle free and untouched by the sultry summer sun. She depicted their leisure time spent with children and wives or lovers, playing sports and going to posh getaway spots, and evenings spent at more meetings, charity events and parties.

She strained her imagination to picture Brian in this life where everything was so expected and pat, ordered and predictable, but she couldn't. He wouldn't have fit in her study. And she couldn't put her finger on why.

Her thoughts ran out then, and she concentrated on getting to the pond. "Are you still with me, Brian?" She looked over her shoulder. Of course he was. Although he was keeping his word and being quiet, his presence was as obvious to her as if she'd been followed by a tribe of banshees.

"I'm right here behind you," Brian said, his eyes never leaving the appealing curves of Sydney's back, "and absolutely entranced by the grace of the female body walking along a Vermont trail."

Sydney quickened her pace. At least he couldn't see her blush from behind. And why was she blushing, anyway? Damn, she'd heard men comment far more graphically on the female body and had handled it just fine. And she'd handle Brian Hennesy just fine, too. It was the whole situation that was throwing her, and once she got used to the temporary curve her life was taking, she'd be okay.

"Here we are," Sydney said a short while later, taking a turnoff and pushing through a tangle of branches. She lowered her camera bag next to a tall birch tree and shoved her hands deep into the pockets of her long shorts. "This is one of my favorite spots on earth—the pond."

"*The* pond," Brian mused, looking off into the clear waters. It was perfectly still, except for an occasional splash from an invisible swamp dweller. There were trees on either side of them, and on the far side of the pond more trees slanted upward as they steadily climbed the mountain. Their sturdy trunks created a fortress around the small scooped-out area that nested quietly in the middle of maple, birch and pine. There were no rafts or docks or piers, only a huge, smooth rock that rose out of the water and looked like the back of a giant gray turtle.

"There's a lake over that way." Sydney pointed to her left as she took a step on the narrow root-laced stretch of land. "But the pond has more atmosphere, I think. I love it here. It's spring fed, so it's cold but clean. Gus used to tell us when we were little that even the mud on the bottom was clean." She leaned down, slipped a brown leather pack from her shoulder to the ground and pulled it open.

"May I see?" Brian bent over beside her, peering into the dark disarray of her bag.

"Sure. Tools of my trade," she said proudly, pulling out lenses of various shapes and sizes.

As he asked about each piece of equipment his interest seemed to form a comfortable web around them.

"Have you ever taken pictures?" Sydney asked.

"Never. I don't think I see things that way. Framed and isolated. I look at a scene and see too many things that aren't there—motives, angles, relationships."

"The birth of a business deal."

"Right." He laughed softly, surprised at her quick understanding. "When you do that twenty-four hours a day, you eventually begin doing it wherever you are—parties, restaurants, ponds. You look at life like that, full of connections—"

Sydney shook her head, uncomfortable with the concept. "That's all too complicated, Brian. You can't do that here. This place is so simple and lovely. There's plenty here all by itself." She closed her eyes and breathed in the pungent air, and a smile lifted the corners of her mouth.

Brian watched her. It *was* simple and lovely, and so was she. He looked around at the thick stand of trees, at the light shimmering on the water, then up toward the mountain in the distance. When he did, his mind shifted slowly, automatically, almost against his will. Yes, it was lovely. A perfect place for a resort. And shops. And only a few acres of woods would have to be cleared, so the natural terrain wouldn't be destroyed. In two years the investment would—

Sydney opened her eyes and looked up into his faraway gaze. He was smiling, pleased at something. "You see, Brian, it's magic out here."

He blinked away the vision and looked down at her, uncomfortable and slightly guilty that the simpleness of what she saw had slipped away from him so quickly. "Yes, it's a nice place. I'm not used to this, I guess—this quiet."

Her throaty laugh charmed him and pushed away the thoughts of deals and land values.

"I know," she said, fitting a long lens on her black camera. "Sometimes when I return from the city it takes me a while to shake off the commotion and chaos. But it never takes long. Here. Would you hold this, please?"

She handed him a lens cap. He held it flat between his palms, his eyes on her movements, watching her watch the land. Now what did she see? he wondered, following the lens of her camera as it slowly explored the wavy perimeter of the pond. Toward the opposite edge, a patch of grasses shimmered above the water's surface, and scampering things could be seen through the green and brown blades when they separated.

"See there, Brian?" She looked up at him with delight shining in her eyes.

He looked again, focusing on the grasses.

"It's a harlequin duck," she whispered, moving closer to the edge of the pond, her camera poised. "A male, I think. See the long tail? This is part of their migratory flight, but they're not very common, so you don't often see them."

Brian strained his eyes and leaned forward beside her. He could see movement but not much else. "Through the grasses?"

She nodded, excited. "I've seen them just a couple of times before, but I've never caught them on film. They're very shy, but so lovely when they take flight. It looks like an Escher print when they all soar in a line and the sun catches that wonderful diamond design on their heads. Shhh—" There was giddy delight in her movements, and Brian shaded his eyes to catch a glimpse of whatever was filling her with such pleasure.

He took a step closer and leaned in the direction of the grasses.

And in that split second, the quiet air was filled with a blinding fusion of sounds: a clicking camera, a flapping of wings and a resounding, echoing splash as Brian Hennesy dived clumsily and heavily into the pond.

"Brian!" Sydney leaped to her feet.

"Damn!" came the forceful answer. It was muted only by the sounds of his body fighting against the shallow water.

He rotated himself slowly around until he was facing Sydney, his body waist deep in swirling waters, his arms braced at his sides and the rest of him a distorted line beneath the water. A continuous stream of water dripped from his hair and face and made widening circles in front of him.

"Oh...Brian," Sydney began. She was afraid to speak, afraid the laughter building in her throat would erupt like a volcano and drown him.

"Is...that...it? *Oh, Brian?*" His mouth was tight and the words came out in a flattened monotone.

Sydney bit down hard on her bottom lip and forced the laughter back. "I... May I help you?" She slipped the camera from around her neck and tucked it safely inside her pack, then took a step toward Brian.

"You certainly may." He held out one muddy hand and leaned his dripping body toward her.

"Of course," she said, wishing she could step back for just two seconds and snap some pictures first. No, that would never do. The expression on Brian's face, interesting as it was, might quite possibly break the camera.

"Here—" She leaned toward him and grasped his hand. Mud squeezed out between their joined fingers.

But before she could fasten her grasp and tug him forward, Brian's other hand rose and grabbed her lower arm. And in one swift jerk, her body flew through the air until it landed with all the force of her one hundred and twenty-two pounds on top of Brian Hennesy.

"What the..." she sputtered as water sprayed into her wide, round mouth.

"I didn't want to be selfish about the experience," a calm voice explained as his arms held her tight against his chest.

"You—" Sydney choked as she wiped wet hair from her eyes and strained to lift herself away from him. She seemed stuck there, her legs wedged between his and her own weight pressing her breasts flat against the hard wall of his chest. With great force she lifted her chin and stared up into his face.

The mixture of laughter and mischief that flowed from his eyes startled her. "You're crazy," she managed to mutter through the tiny space between them.

"You were the one who proclaimed this your favorite spot on earth." Brian watched the gold specks in her eyes. They were dancing like sunlit dust beneath her feeble attempt at anger.

"I didn't mean exactly *here*," she said shakily. He was so close she could hardly breathe. They might as well have been pressed together naked for all the good her thin, soaked T-shirt and his cotton shirt were doing them. There was a gracious way out of this, she suspected, but damned if they'd taught it at Radcliffe!

"Hey," Brian whispered into the wet strands of hair looped over her ear, "be still for a moment, all right?" If she moved one more time he was going to have great difficulty getting out of the pond intact. His reaction was spontaneous, but considering the effect Sydney had had on him from day one, it should have been expected. "Maybe if we think about this for a minute, it will make more sense."

"I doubt it."

"You're probably right." There, he'd managed to move one leg enough to decrease the pressure, and Sydney was balanced sideways, one shoulder pressing lightly against his chest and his arm supporting her back. But the gentle lap at his nerve endings was still present, and it was enough to make him wonder how he'd gotten this far in life without ever falling into a pond. "You were right about the water, Sydney. It is cold."

"Thank God!" Her blunt statement startled them both for a moment, and then their laughter erupted together and traveled over the still water, releasing the tension.

"But it's clean," Sydney said, her heart still pounding fiercely.

"Even the mud?" He lifted her hand, which was still tightly grasped in his own. Light brown plops of mud squeezed out from between their fingers and dropped down onto the soggy cotton of his shirt. "Yep, clean as a whistle."

Sydney shook her head, and the water from her hair lightly sprayed the air about them. "People come from miles around for this mud."

"That's good to know," Brian murmured. She felt absolutely delicious there in his arms, and the water surrounding them was conducting something far more interesting than electricity. He could feel it in her, too—the instant reaction, the pleasure in their bodies touching, the keen awareness of each other. It was a sweet joining that was far deeper than simple sexual desire.

"We really ought to—" Sydney began reluctantly, then stopped short when movement from behind Brian caught her eye. She looked toward the far edges of the pond.

"Brian, look!" She lifted one hand from the water and pointed over his shoulder.

He shifted his body on the soft bottom of the pond until he could see where she pointed. The grasses across the pond were waving more wildly now, and from their bases a sweep of reddish-black color and flapping wings rose.

"The harlequins!"

"Fantastic," Brian whispered, his mind taking in the scene. The deep sky was filled with movement of the long-tailed ducks moving steadily up into the sky. Brian and Sydney watched together in silence until the solid band of birds disappeared over the thick bank of evergreen trees.

"I'd like to follow them," Brian said softly, his eyes still focused on the distant, deepening sky.

Sydney nodded. "I know. I always feel that way. Someday I will."

Brian watched the soft beauty of her face. It seemed to absorb and mirror the naturalness around them, the incredible vision of the migrating birds, the spring-fed pond with the waving sentinel of trees protecting them from everything else in the world, the sweetness of their bodies touching.

"We probably look pretty silly—" Sydney's words came falteringly.

"To the ducks?" He lifted a band of her silky wet hair and let the shining strands fall through his fingers.

"And mountain elves. Woodchucks. The raccoons. All those guys." Her mind was about the same consistency as the soft, cushiony mud she sat on. "We need to dry off before the sun disappears completely. Come on." Before fate played any other tricks on her, Sydney pushed herself up to her knees.

"And just when my niche was perfectly carved in the mud. I was considering squatter's rights."

The teasing midnight-blue eyes swept over her, and Sydney felt the hardness of her nipples pressing against the tissue-thin T-shirt. "Not today, Hennesy. Come on—" she splashed cold water on his chest and then on her legs, rubbing free the mud that clung to the backs of them "—clean off the mud and then we can dry off on the rock over there."

She scampered out of the lake quickly and managed to pluck the T-shirt away from her skin enough to disguise her near nakedness. "Make sure your shoes are in a sunny spot," she called back as she pulled herself up onto the large boulder.

"You sound like you've done this before," he said, removing the heavy, soggy Topsiders and placing them next to her tennis shoes.

"Oh, often." Sydney stretched herself out on the warm flatness of the rock. "But usually it's been of my own free will."

Brian climbed up beside her, then began unbuttoning his soaking shirt. "Who with?"

"Who with what?" The shadow of his upright body fell across her, and she watched from beneath it as he peeled off his shirt and dropped it beside him on the boulder.

He turned his head and looked down at her, a boyish smile appearing in the shadow. "Who else have you gone swimming with here?"

Sydney's mind was busy recording the solid mass of coarse, dark hair that coated the muscles of his chest. Dampness still clung to the springy strands of hair, and they glistened when he moved. She wondered about touching them, feeling the tiny drops of water that settled there like morning dew on the grass. A knot pulled tight deep inside her.

"A man, maybe?" Brian stretched out beside her and folded his arms behind his head.

"A man?" Sydney blinked. "Oh, swimming! No, no man. Boys, maybe, when I was little. But now I'm very selfish about this spot. I come here alone—" She breathed in slowly and looked up at the deepening sky. *Until today, that is.* She was definitely not alone today. The long length of Brian's body beside her own was there as solid, living proof. He wasn't touching her, although they were lined up so closely she could feel the drying heat of him and could hear the relaxed sound of his breathing.

The fading rays of sunlight flattened against her body and tugged free the nervousness of her thoughts. *Poof,* she thought, *go away.* It was too lovely a day to feel tension. When she closed her eyes she could still see the bright blur of the sun and the shadowy smile of Brian's face when he'd looked down. The two images melted together.

"You're smiling." Brian's voice entered her world, and it, too, joined with the floating image.

"Humpf," she said.

"And you should be furious."

Sydney half opened one eye. He had lifted himself on one elbow and was looking down at her. "Yes."

"Because I barged in on your private place."

"No, because you made me lose an excellent shot of the ducks taking flight. You owe me a big one for that. But as for being here—" She smiled slowly. "I invited you. And I have no earthly idea why, but I did it. You know, I didn't plan on liking you, Brian Hennesy."

"And do you?" His smile was crooked and beguiling. A pleased smile. He played with a strand of her damp hair.

"I don't know for sure. I like parts of you—"

Brian looked down at his bare chest, then slowly canvassed her lean, stretched-out body. "I like parts of you, too, Sydney. Very much, in fact." *All* parts of her, the long graceful curve of her neck, the creamy rise of her breasts beneath the damp T-shirt, the arch of her hips and the firm flatness of her stomach.

It would have been far easier to ignore a herd of elephants than the tickling fingers of sensation his words caused, but Sydney gave it a valiant try. "You don't follow a blueprint, and that confuses me, Brian. You...you're a hard-nosed business man. I saw it in your face when you bid at the auction."

Brian nodded and ran his finger down the side of her face. "You're right. There is that part of me. I worked hard at developing it, as a matter of fact. I'm sorry you don't like it."

But his gentle smile wasn't that of a hardened businessman, and a small sigh escaped from Sydney. "See? That's where you mess it up—the nice way you laugh and the look in your eyes." It was far too dangerous to describe that in more detail, so Sydney simply paused for a moment, then continued in a slight rush of words. "If a calculating, inndemolishing businessman is what you are, then act like it all the time and don't show me other sides of you that I like. It makes it all too confusing."

Brian's husky laughter was warm and gentle, and Sydney found herself smiling at it. "I sound terribly narrow, don't I?"

He nodded, his fingers still tracing rivulets down across her cheeks and neck. "Maybe the problem is that we really don't know each other. All we know is that we're terribly attracted to each other and that I'm trying to make a deal that will tear down an inn you love, and you're trying to save it. Which, by the way, I admire like hell."

He leaned over a little more, and Sydney could see in his eyes that he meant what he said. "Why are you not fighting me on this? You could have stopped it; you know that as well as I do. You could have bought the inn last week—"

Brian shrugged. Should he tell her he was benefiting from her heroic gesture? It seemed so crass and harsh, somehow, in the light of the clear waters and lovely day, and so unnecessary. His motivation certainly wouldn't affect the outcome. He looked out over the pond. "A month isn't going to hurt anything. And it's giving me a nice vacation, just as you pointed out."

"You don't take vacations often, I suspect."

"Not recently."

"How recently?"

"Oh, twenty years or so."

"Not since you were a kid?"

He nodded. "And even then we didn't really go on trips. We'd go to my grandparents' farm and help them out for a week or so in the summer."

"So you're not completely city?"

Sydney's voice lifted with the words, as if Brian had just told her something wonderful about himself. He laughed. "No, there's a bit of straw behind my ears. It's several years old, though."

"Did you like it? Your time in the country?"

Brian was silent as he pondered the question, then answered thoughtfully, "Yes, I did. I think I liked the outdoors. I liked wading in streams and milking the cows and running free. But I knew even then, when I spun out crazy dreams the way kids do, that I didn't want that kind of life when I grew up.''

"Why?'' she asked quietly.

"It was a poor life, Sydney. We lived in a run-down section of Philadelphia, and I wanted more than that. I was a smart kid and knew my intelligence could get me out. And it did. I had the navy put me through school, did a hitch for Uncle Sam, then settled down to taking the financial world by storm and making lots of money.''

"That sounds so...''

"Crass? Yeah, I guess it does.'' He pinched a fold of her T-shirt together and peeled it slowly from her skin. It formed a white cushiony bubble, then slowly flattened against her peach-colored skin. Brian watched it with pleasure, then left his fingers there, just above her breast, rubbing lightly on the thin, damp fabric. "But I think it's more crass in the retelling than it actually was. I loved my parents, and I think I hung on to the values they taught me when I moved into the wicked world of business. If you'd been along on the way from there to here you'd see it wasn't all materialistic fervor.'' He smiled at that last thought and said, "Now *that* would have been nice—having you along on the ride.''

"Hmm,'' Sydney said, her eyes half closing, her mind accepting the compliment easily. "Let me imagine what it was like from there to here. Boy genius from blue-collar neighborhood astounds teachers at Ivy League college—''

"Penn State, actually, but the rest sounds okay.''

"Correction accepted. After the necessary military time, during which said genius probably managed to establish himself as a wunderkind by investing sailors' meager pennies in foreign markets—''

"New York Stock Exchange. Very traditional in certain ways, this boy genius....'' His fingers slipped beneath the neck of her T-shirt and rubbed gently against the wet, slippery skin.

Sydney felt his touch somewhere far deeper than her skin, but she managed to lie still on the surface of the rock. She continued, her voice dropping slightly and her words spreading apart. "Our boy genius by this time is a young man. A very successful young man—"

"Only to his family at this point. It took two or three years for the financial community to acknowledge me publicly. I was an upstart of sorts, and there weren't any notable Hennesys on any boards that mattered."

Sydney nodded dreamily, the scenario playing before her eyes while the sun and Brian's fingers soothed her body into a wonderfully free state. "And at some point on this journey, such a man of which we speak must have been attracted to a bevy of lovely women waiting in the wings to devote themselves to furthering his career—"

"I don't know about that. This fellow, you see, was so goal directed in his career he didn't waste time looking for a partner of that sort. That would have been far too time-consuming and distracting a project for this single-minded chap."

"Funny, you don't look like a monk."

"Well, there are casual relationships that, uh, go with the territory, so to speak. And they seem to have sufficed."

Sydney raised one eye. "A playboy—I should have known."

Brian's eyes were gentle as he looked down at her, and she could feel the smile in his voice. "Nah, not so you'd notice. Playboys spend a hell of a lot of time doing what they do. I simply have some women friends, acquaintances. And they don't expect a lot of me. They understand I'm not at the top of the ladder yet—"

"And what will be there waiting for you at the top, Brian?"

"I haven't quite figured that out yet. Fame. Riches. Glory. Another mountain. Who knows? The woman of my dreams, maybe?" Brian's caressing fingers moved as slowly as his words. He felt it again, that enchantment, that witchery. Or whatever it was about Sydney Hanover that pushed aside rational thought and replaced it with this soft foreign sensation of lying on a cloud and spinning dreams.

Beneath his touch Sydney shivered but didn't move. She was busy sorting through the dreamlike threads that wove a portrait of the woman of Brian's dreams. The image refused to come. "Well, when you find her," she said, the words struggling forth from deep in her throat, "how will she fit into this world of yours—your ambition, your goals?"

Brian pressed his lids together momentarily and fought to concentrate on her words. He wanted to kiss her, to slip his arms beneath her and mold her beautiful body to his. She looked so incredibly sexy stretched out on the rock in that nearly transparent shirt, her shorts molded to her thighs in a way that invited his touch. The desire to make sweet, magical love to her right there on the warm, flat rock swelled up from every channel of his body, and it seemed as natural and basic as the migrating ducks and the setting sun and the clear, cool water of the pond.

"Brian, what...are...you...doing?" Sydney pulled her lids opened and stared into the wall of his chest.

"I can't help myself. It's the wet T-shirt." His fingers slipped beneath the drooping neckline and snaked downward until he felt the rise and fall of her breasts beneath them. "Or maybe it was the ducks. Migrating and all—"

Sydney tore her eyes from his chest where she was beginning to fantasize all sorts of tantalizing things that had nearly nothing to do with migrating ducks. "Brian, if I might say something here," she said, choking.

"It depends."

His fingers continued to draw heated trails across her breasts and she struggled with her self-control. Balance, Sydney old girl, her mind said in a meaningless singsong. With great effort she pushed herself up on her elbows.

Brian's hand moved with her, his fingers finding delight in her movement and the new curves to explore.

Sydney bit down hard on her lip and forced calm into parts of her body that had awakened with a vengeance. "Stop it, Brian," she said softly, grasping his wrist with her fingers and tugging it free of her shirt.

Brian lifted his head and saw the intensity in her large eyes. There was something else there, too. It wasn't fear, exactly, but a kind of vulnerability that made him pause. He had missed it before beneath her self-assured manner, but there it was, a softening in those lovely eyes, a caution. With new gentleness he slid one arm behind her and pulled her up beside him. "I'm sorry, Sydney. I guess I did get carried away there."

"No problem, Brian. I was enjoying it, too, as you undoubtedly could tell. But somehow it doesn't seem like the right course of action right now, don't you agree?" She tossed her damp hair carelessly and slipped a smile across her face, but her casual actions failed to hide the shakiness in her voice.

Brian looked at her intently, but his voice was gentle. "No, I don't agree, Sydney. I guess I believe in separation of business and pleasure, but there's no business going on here. So I don't see why we can't enjoy each other, especially since it seems such a mutually agreeable thing to do."

"Well, because we can't, that's all." Sydney cringed at her own silly answer. Her impulse was to attack Brian Hennesy, to pull him close to her and let the lovely warmth of his body seep right into her pores. But she couldn't, of course. Moving from the frying pan to the fire wasn't in the plan. The thought broadened and loosened her careful smile.

Brian felt her muscles relax beneath his palm. "And that makes you smile?"

"No, comparing you to a frying pan makes me smile."

"I guess I wasn't aware we'd done that." Brian hadn't the faintest notion what she was talking about, but nonsense beat the slight chill he had felt a minute ago. "What kind of pan: cast-iron?"

"Teflon. No-stick. But you're not the frying pan. Stan was. We were engaged for three years. You're the fire I don't want to jump into. And if we want to stretch the metaphor, I suppose a forest fire would be appropriate."

"Good, I approve." Brian kept his eyes on her face, trying to digest the three-year engagement news and wondering why the information mattered so much. "About the Teflon pan—"

Sydney rubbed a small knot on the surface of the rock. "Stan Woolfe lives in New York, and he and I were engaged for a long time. Finally we both realized we didn't want to marry. So we broke the engagement. It's nothing that hasn't happened before."

"To you?"

"No—" she laughed "—in the universe. I mean it's not an unusual story."

But it was, Brian argued silently, because it had to do with her. And for reasons that he couldn't quite come to grips with, anything that had to do with Sydney mattered now and was unusual and unique. "Why did you break the engagement, Sydney?"

She looked at him sideways. "How do you know *I* broke it?"

"Because no man in his right mind would walk away from you."

His voice had grown a shade more husky, and Sydney shifted uncomfortably on the rock. "Well, thank you, Brian. But you don't know me very well. Stan was equally happy with the arrangement." She flashed a small smile.

"Good. Then there's no broken heart floating around to impose guilt on you."

"The only thing imposing guilt on me is the fact that somehow, while you were distracting me, the sun slipped clear out of the sky and took with it my workday."

He followed her gaze and was surprised at the dusky splendor that had crept up on them. An invisible hand had painted the distant sky with broad sweeping strokes of reds and purples and deep blues. The water beneath it shimmered with the deepening colors.

"It's beautiful," he said softly.

She nodded beside him, lost for a moment in the dying glory of the day.

The sweet-smelling pine woods siphoned any worldly sounds except for the nightly cry of the invisible crickets calling for their mates, and the slow rhythmic lapping of the water against the shore.

They sat together, as still as the harlequin ducks before they'd filled the sky with their movement. Speaking would have ruined the moment, but Sydney sensed something else: their silence was allowing the connecting threads between them to strengthen. She curled her fingers tightly around the edge of the rock. "Brian, it's time—"

"Shhh . . ." He lifted a finger to her lips.

In the distance the crickets grew louder, but their love sounds were mixed now with the crackling of leaves and the snapping of pine needles being pressed into the earth.

"We're being invaded," he whispered.

"Yoo-hoo! You-all here?" The deep familiar voice cut through the dusk, and Sydney watched as the magic before her separated into thin strips and then disappeared.

"Hi, Gus. We're over here."

The old man stepped clear of the trees and focused on the two still figures silhouetted against the darkening sky. "Got a piece of the rock, hey?"

Brian and Sydney moaned at his bad pun as Gus and Mo, a brown-spotted mutt who loved Gus more than raw steak, approached them.

"Hi, Gus," Brian said halfheartedly. He wasn't sure what could have followed. He and Sydney had moved around each other in some sort of dance, coming close and moving apart. But he hated to have it come to a stop, even for a while.

"I was worried about you two," Gus said loudly, scattering the silence. "Sydney knows this land nearly as well as I

do, but you never know what can happen. I watch out for
my folks, like I said—''

He stepped closer and scrutinized their attire. "Looks to
me like it rained out here. Funny how we didn't get any back
at the inn.''

"Real funny, Gus." Sydney slipped gracefully from the
rock and walked barefoot to her shoes. "Brian decided to
go swimming, and I had to save him.''

"In three feet of pond water?''

"You know these city slickers, Gus." Sydney squeezed
into her shoes and watched the pond water ooze out through
the laces.

"That's what she tells you." Brian slipped into his shirt
and joined them at the path. "In actual fact, what happened is far too personal to relate in mixed company.'' He
glanced down solemnly at Mo.

Mo thumped an unkempt tail on the ground, and Brian
reached down and scratched him behind an ear.

"Actually," Gus shifted from one foot to the other, "I
came out on business.''

"What kind of business, Gus?" Brian tugged on his
Topsiders and picked up Sydney's camera pack.

"Well, uh, for Sydney." He looked from one to the other,
then, realizing he wasn't going to get to talk to her pri-
vately, plunged in. "Don Hendricks—he's my lawyer—
stopped by your house, Sydney, and Hortense sent him over
to the inn.''

"Why?" Sydney's eyes widened.

"Oh, nothing to worry your beautiful head about. He's
got all those papers of intent to purchase put together and
needs your John Henry, that's all." Gus threw Brian an
apologetic glance.

Sydney watched the discomfort on Gus's face. "Gus
Ahern, stop that!" Sydney clamped her fists down hard on
her hips, amused irritation flashing in her green eyes. "Why
are you acting so embarrassed about this? For heaven's

sake, don't act like you're going to hurt Brian's feelings. He's the *bad* guy in this deal.''

"Bad guy, huh?" Brian drummed his fingers along her shoulder. "We'll see about that. But she's right, Gus. Don't be uncomfortable. We all know where we stand." His eyes moved slowly from Sydney to Gus and back to Sydney. They settled there unnervingly.

"Where's that?" she asked Brian as Gus turned toward the shadowy woods and beckoned them to follow.

Brian didn't answer for a moment. Instead he began to gently massage the tired muscles of her back as she turned and started along the path. Instantly she felt her nerves react and her mind haze over, and she wasn't at all sure where she stood. Mars was a distinct possibility.

His blunt fingers pressed and rubbed rhythmically, responding to her body's need. Brian bent his head lower until his cheek rubbed against her head. "Where do we stand?" he asked huskily, whispering the words into her hair. "In pond-drenched shoes on shaky land, my darlin'. And I'm not sure when it will all dry up."

Five

After the Afternoon of the Rock, which is how Sydney came to think of it in her mind, life took a turn for its most hectic worst.

Alana Spencer, Sydney's mother, called from Bermuda and announced she was going to sail for Majorca but might perhaps come to Vermont first to say ciao and make sure her darling was all right.

Her father called to say he heard she was tapping all their friends for money, and although he was okay with the idea—they could well afford it—he thought she ought to slow down a bit. What was she doing with it, anyway?

And Brian Hennesy was settling into life at Candlewick Inn as if he meant to stay a long time.

"How can anyone intent on tearing a place apart *live* in it the way he is?" she wondered aloud as she and Grams sat together at the kitchen table. The cool, rational voice inside her head was operating on full circuit today. Sydney had left strict instructions. It was more comfortable to deal with

Brian this way, as a kind of foe with whom she could be ir-ritated. At least when she wasn't with him, she found it easier to control the havoc churning inside of her."

"How's that, sweet pea? How is he living in it?"

"So...so comfortably. He's enjoying it, Grams. Gus says Brian is fascinated with the way the inn is run: he seems obsessed with the cook's flapjacks and brought her flowers this week; the girls who clean the guest rooms love him. He leaves enormous tips, he helps Gus with desk work, he—he's being so *inappropriate*." She shuffled the stack of papers in front of her and tossed it down on the table.

Grams smiled, nodding her head.

"Now what's that for? Why are you smiling?" Sydney glared at her across the kitchen table.

"It isn't a surprise that the girls love him, is what I was thinking. And it made me smile."

"You like him, too, don't you? You traitor."

Grams chuckled merrily. "You can't fool me, Sydney Spencer Hanover. You're a little twitchy yourself, and it's not from this inn thing. Challenges never did this to you, young lady, no sirree. It's more as if you've been caught on a moonbeam and don't know how to get off."

"You're saying I'm loony? Maybe you're right."

"I'm saying the young fellow has your pulse dancing, Sydney."

"He's not so young. He's thirty-five."

Grams scoffed. "When I was thirty-five, I was young."

"All right, I like him. He's a charmer. And he's trying to charm me." Sydney slapped a stamp on an envelope. "Why not? Why shouldn't he charm me? I'm a worthy charmee—I'm intelligent and reasonably good-looking."

"Reasonably? Dearie, you have the Spencer nose and coloring. Hair of many colors. You're beautiful, just like your Great-Aunt Sylvia, except she didn't care much for herself, poor soul." Grams traveled off on a winding, vague history of Sylvia Spencer's downfall due to curious overindulgences.

Sydney packed up her pile of letters, listening with half an ear. But her mind had already boomeranged back to the enigma of Brian Hennesy. The feelings he lighted in her weren't ordinary; she'd been around enough men to know that. And those feelings grew like a forest fire every time they were together. It was the kind of thing she had *hoped* would happen with Stanley—that they would grow together through time. Yet in two weeks Brian had leaped way beyond any record Stan had set in three years. And she knew the end was not even in sight. And she hardly knew the man. She suspected there were large chunks of him she wouldn't like as well as the parts sweeping her off her feet, but those parts seemed hidden away these days, right along with his three-piece suit. She almost wished he'd start wearing it again. It would be a nice reminder of the way things really were.

She looked up to see her grandmother heading out the back door. "Grams, where are you going?"

"To the barn. I misplaced something. Need to look for it, sweet pea."

"What? Maybe I can help."

Grams paused and looked intently at the wide-planked floor. When she looked up there was a hazy, faraway look in her eye. "No. You be about your business of buying the inn, Sydney. That's your job now."

Sydney rose from the chair and walked over to Grams. She wrapped an arm around her thin shoulders and squeezed her carefully. "Are you all right, darling? You look tired."

Grams lifted her fingers to her cheek and pushed in distractedly on the loose, lined skin. "No, I'm not tired. I'm just busy, that's all. Finding things, you know."

Sydney shook her head. "Will you be okay, Grams? You know I'm driving down to New York today. I'll probably be back sometime tomorrow."

Grams lifted her small face and pressed her brows together sternly. "Certainly, dear. I'm a Spencer, don't forget. And I've lived—"

"—alone for twenty years," Sydney continued by rote, a smile easing the trace of worry she'd felt. "And you're right, you do fine, but I do wish you'd let me hire one of the girls from the village to stay here."

"Well, I won't, so you scat now and be about your business. And I'll see you next week."

"Tomorrow, Grams."

"That's even better." She pecked Sydney on the cheek and slipped out the door.

Sydney watched her through the back window until she disappeared inside the freshly painted barn. It was only used now for storage, although the hayloft remained intact and was always filled with fresh hay—for the mice and kitty cats, Grams insisted—and Sydney dutifully saw to it that fat bales of hay were delivered every few months.

"Dear, sweet Grams," she murmured into the lilac-smelling air, her eyes filling unexpectedly with misty affection. She almost followed Grams out, just to be near her for another moment, but the front door chimed, distracting her and drawing her to the front of the house.

She opened the door to a huge cardboard box that nearly blocked out the morning light.

"Wh-what?" Sydney stepped back and the box took on perspective. It wasn't standing on the threshold alone. There were arms, legs and feet in all the expected places.

"Hi, Sydney." Brian leaned to one side of the cardboard box and smiled.

Sydney's face lighted. "Brian, hi. Who's your friend?"

"You'll soon see. And both of us would greatly appreciate an invitation to set this down in your front hallway."

"I'm sorry. Of course." Sydney stepped quickly aside while Brian eased the package down to the floor.

"This, lovely Sydney, is for you."

Sydney looked from the box to his face and tried to figure out the gesture. Was it a joke? Should she laugh lightly and pull out the contents, maybe a goat or a plastic flamingo or a giant papier-mâché ham steak? Or should she looked pleased yet reticent?

She hoped fiercely it was something light and joking that they could both handle easily and distantly.

"Well?" Brian leaned his head to one side, his tan brow wrinkled. "What's up? You look like you're analyzing every inch of cardboard and staple. It won't bite, Sydney; go on, open it."

Sydney held her bottom lip between her teeth for one minute of thought, then knelt down and began to pull back the flaps of the box. Inside was a mound of crushed newspaper.

"Come on, come on," Brian said, leaning over her shoulder and pulling out handfuls of paper. "They'll suffocate."

Sydney narrowed her eyes and strained back to see his face. "Hennesy..."

He ran a finger along the hairline on the side of her face. "Where's your sense of adventure?"

Sydney slipped free of his touch and again attacked the box, wiggling her fingers through the crumpled masses of newsprint until they struck a form. It was feathery and solid, and she jerked her hand back instantly.

"I can see we need to work on trust here," Brian said with amusement. "Here, darlin'—" He leaned over her shoulder and dug in until he grabbed on to the hard form. Carefully he pulled out a feathery object and held it in front of her.

Sydney stared. Then slowly she reached out and touched it. It was a beautiful wooden replica of a harlequin duck, so exact in every detail from the bluish-black feathers gracing the curved body to the glossy, partly opened beak, that she had the eerie sensation it was going to flap its breathtaking wings and take flight. She looked up and stared at Brian.

"That's not all." He reached in and pulled out three more, each lifelike in every detail but differing slightly from the others in such details as the cast of the midnight glass eyes, the settling of the feathers or the placement of the white design on its head. "Birds of a feather, you know."

"Oh, my—" she breathed.

"It's your flock. A temporary replacement until they come back. I spent the past three days combing craft shops for someone who could do justice to their beauty."

"You found someone, that's certain." She stroked the tips of the feathers with one finger. They were as silky smooth as the down of a goose.

"Herman Farley, over in Newfane, makes these. He does it all by hand. By the way, I promised him one of your photos when you finally do catch the flock on film."

Sydney smiled.

"He does a terrific job, don't you think? There was a fellow in Readsboro who had the real thing, as stuffed and elegant looking as Thanksgiving turkeys. But I can't quite handle that—the real thing but not so real anymore."

"No, I can't either," she said softly. "But these are truly works of art."

"Good. Now you can have your own flock sitting on your windowsill for the winter. They don't completely make up for the mess I made of the day, but maybe they'll help."

"I wouldn't call that day a mess, exactly," Sydney said slowly, her eyes focusing on the gorgeous play of colors across one of the birds' backs.

Brian leaned against the door frame, hands comfortably slipped into his slacks pockets, and smiled. "No, I wouldn't, either, not really. It was one of the nicest afternoons I've had in a very long time."

Sydney looked up. It was clear in his voice that he meant it. But when she looked at his face and her gaze lingered on the darkening circle of his eyes, something else was clear— a desire so rich and flowing that she knew she'd be able to touch it if she lifted her hand just an inch.

She sat back on her bent legs and held a duck close to her chest. It gave faint comfort beneath his steady gaze. "You know, Hennesy, there's one thing that amazes me," she managed shakily.

"What's that?"

"How can anyone do serious, megabucks business when he or she is dealing with someone who has X-rated eyes?"

Brian's husky laugh helped her to her feet. "That's the nicest thing you've said to me today. Now say yes to lunch and it will be the second nicest."

"Lunch?"

"Ham steaks at the Widow's place, or Gus's cook, Jennie, makes a fantastic chicken-salad croissant. What's your pleasure?"

For unclear reasons the mention of her lifelong ties with such familiarity brought a cool rush of air, and Sydney felt reality stepping in. "I know about Jennie's chicken salad." The words sounded defensive. Quickly she added, "You know, Brian, you're beginning to sound like you live here."

Brian reached out and touched Sydney's cheek. He found himself wanting to do that more and more—to touch her, be close to her, feel the warmth she generated and smell the sweet soapy fragrance of her skin and hair. "And that somehow disturbs you, Sydney. Why?"

"Well, because you don't have the right to fit in and enjoy this town, Brian."

"The inn," he said simply.

Sydney set the wooden forms back into the bed of paper and carefully pushed the box against the wall. "Lunch is out, anyway. I have to be away for a day or so for business meetings, and I'm leaving soon. In fact, I'm late now." She stood and turned toward the door.

"Now that's a brush-off if I ever heard one," Brian said gently.

Sydney looked down at the box and touched the corner with the toe of her tennis shoe. This wasn't Brian's problem, it was *hers*, and she was dealing with it about as deftly as she'd dealt with her parents' life-style when she was seven. That year she'd staunchly informed her class at Saint Cecilia's that all *mature* people lived the way her parents did, and anyone who disagreed was uninvited to her birthday party and could go suck eggs. Now here she was uninviting Brian into her life. She looked up slowly. "I'm sorry, Brian. I didn't mean it to sound that way. I have a lot of things on my mind, is all...."

Of course she did, Brian knew, because he did, too. And it was an unlikely mixture of things that didn't sit well together—cold business details side by side with an enormous sexual attraction that deepened by the second. And if that weren't enough, Sydney had an emotional attachment to Candlewick Inn to deal with as well. "Sure, I understand. Well, I guess I'd better be off."

"I do appreciate the birds, Brian. They're absolutely beautiful."

"You can look at them and think of flying off—"

"Or of a nice man plunging into the cold waters of Candlewick Pond."

He grinned. "Sure. And don't forget the rest of that day, either." He leaned over and drew her close. Then, before she had time to think, he kissed her lightly on the lips and was gone.

Brian sat in La Chantilly restaurant on East Fifty-Seventh Street and sipped his martini. His two associates, Jim Goodlin, a vice president from the Goodlin Group, and a lawyer named Justin Fibbard conversed animatedly about the plans for the Vermont shopping-resort area.

Brian thought of Sydney.

The news that she wasn't going to be around for a couple of days had somehow given him the impetus he'd needed to come into the city and have an overdue meeting with clients. Greenbriar was still a lovely little town, restful in an unexpected sort of way. But without Sydney there it was easy to leave.

She had said she was going away on business. It must have
been to see bankers and to try to collect money for the inn.
The thought made him feel a twinge of guilt. She was gutsy
and bright, but innocent in so many ways. None of the big
banks would give her money for the project. Goodlin did
business with so many of them that its interests would pro-
hibit a bank from even glancing at Sydney.

He'd stopped himself several times from asking about her
plan. It wouldn't be appropriate, he knew; his instinct was
to help her, and ethically he couldn't do that. And she'd
think, rightfully so, that he was prying. This thirty-day game
was turning out to be damned frustrating, and frankly he'd
be glad when it was over. Except for the fact of Sydney herself. And that was becoming a whole other matter.

"I think he's dead, Brian," Jim Goodlin said.

Brian looked up with a start. "Who?"

"Whomever you're voodooing with that toothpick."

Brian looked down at his massacred cocktail napkin. He
laughed shortly. "Well, that takes care of that, then. Now,
what were you saying?"

"Just that you're next to brilliant for delaying this deal
the way you have. The penalty on calling the note in early
was significant."

"Good. That's what I figured."

"How did you do it, Brian?" Jim Goodlin asked. "I hear
there's a woman involved. Did you bed her around to seeing
things right?"

The other two men laughed heartily, but Brian's chest
constricted beneath the Italian-tailored suit. He clenched his
martini glass with tense fingers and hoped for the sake of the
two men's well-being and health that they shut their mouths.

"Hey, careful, Brian. We need those hands to keep signing deals for us. Now, come on, what's the scoop?"

"No scoop, no sex, no nothing. There's a bright young
woman in Greenbriar who's interested in buying the inn,
that's all. I don't think she can do it, but she's dead serious
about trying and asked for the thirty-day extension herself.

It was pure luck on our part, that's all. No fancy—or lewd—manipulating at all."

His associates nodded, obviously thankful there were gullible women to make their own lives more profitable.

"It's not that way at all." Brian shook his head irritably. "She simply doesn't have the means, that's all. Now can we talk about something else?" Even to his own ears his tone was fierce.

The two men stared at him for a moment. Brian knew he was known for his cool and calm approach in handling business matters, and this was a side of him they hadn't seen before. "Are you getting sick, Brian?" Justin asked.

"I hear there's a rotten flu going around," Jim Goodlin added. "You ought to sack out in Palm Springs for the next couple of weeks and enjoy yourself."

Brian nodded noncommittally and focused his eyes intently on the tall leather menu. Food, that's what he needed. He hadn't had anything to eat since Jennie's flapjacks earlier that day. When Sydney had turned him down for lunch, food lost its appeal, and he'd simply gotten in his car and driven off. He reached for a crusty roll, ordered dill-flavored *noisettes d'agneau* and settled back with tastes and images of the Widow's smoked ham and Sydney Hanover's throaty laugh filling his mind.

"So," Justin Fibbard said a while later, pushing away a delicate porcelain plate that minutes ago had boasted a crisp *feuilleté*, "looks like things are filling out beautifully."

Jim Goodlin eyed the lawyer's empty plate. "Yourself included, Justin. But there's one more thing we need to discuss while we have Brian here."

Brian looked up from his coffee cup.

"There's a huge, useless hunk of land out in Oregon, Brian, that's just itching for some attention. What do you say you take a look after this Vermont deal is sewn up. It's just the sort of thing we could turn into a Disney World kind of gold mine."

"Oregon?" Brian's gaze drifted around the room. Oregon sounded remote, as far away as the moon. Far away from Vermont, anyway. "Well, I'll have to think about it, Jim."

"Think about what? Brian, this is right up your alley."

Brian was finding it hard to concentrate. He didn't want to talk any more business and plan any more deals right now. He wanted to lose himself in the restaurant's misty murals of the grand château at Chantilly and to think about nothing for a while. What a luxury, to think of nothing and simply *be*, like the pond at Candlewick.

A floating mist of silk caught his eye as an elegant woman rose from a table some distance away. He could only see her from behind but the image intrigued him, the daringly low V of her dress caressing the delicate curves of her back and the wash of raw silk the color of a honeydew melon. It floated about her like a misty cloud.

The woman's hair fell to her bare shoulders, a thick, shining blend of many colors. That's what it was that had caught his attention so completely—her hair. It was like Sydney's: multicolored, glistening and free. The woman turned slightly, and Brian watched her profile come into view. And then his heart stopped.

She was a Sydney look-alike. Except for the elegant, sophisticated dress and manner, she could have been Sydney's twin.

Brian stared, trying to pull her into closer view, but they were separated by many tables and the woman came in and out of focus as waiters and diners moved across his line of vision. The space cleared then, and he could see her bend over, see her hair float across her shoulders and along the side of her cheek. She laid one hand on the shoulder of a man, and it wasn't until then that Brian took in the rest of the table. There were two men sitting down, elegantly attired and totally captivated by the woman who stood over them. And as he watched, the woman kissed one man on the cheek, then turned and did the same to the other. The second man rose, not satisfied with the kiss, and embraced her warmly. And then she was gone, disappearing across the plum-colored carpet and out the door.

Before he had time to assess his actions, Brian rose from the table and followed her. He couldn't think of anything, except that Sydney had somehow been transformed into this ethereal mystery woman dining in an elegant restaurant with two attentive suitors. It made him slightly crazy.

When he reached the entryway, he looked between slow-moving patrons and tried to find her. She had disappeared completely. Vanished. He shook his head and tried to recapture the image of the graceful woman bending over the table, but he could see only Sydney, her hair swinging loosely against her shoulders and her easy, luscious charm painting sunshine into his life.

He walked slowly to the table, seriously questioning his sanity. It was an illusion, that was all. And they did say everyone had a double somewhere in the world. Evidently Sydney's was right here in New York.

When Brian found her late the next day, Sydney was standing by a wooden fence bordered by a brilliant parade of wild flowers. There was a stream beyond the fence. Gus's directions had been foolproof.

Brian was exhausted, but the sight of her lifted his spirits. Sleep had been fitful the night before, full of starts and stops and spent in Jim Goodlin's lavish guest room. Both Jim and Justin Fibbard had insisted Brian not spend hours on the road driving back to Vermont, and had also suggested he restrict his intake of liquor for the next few days.

It was easier to laugh and accept their chiding than to try to explain an illusion, so Brian spent the night, then headed north as early as politeness allowed.

And now there she was, standing with her back to him, in familiar jeans and a bright green T-shirt, clean afternoon sunlight pouring over her.

"Sydney?" His voice traveled over the slope of land and down to where she stood beside the fence.

Sydney was motionless for a moment, her camera poised and her attention riveted on something Brian couldn't see. He walked quietly across the grass and stopped at her side.

"Hi," she said softly, as if it were the most natural thing in the world for him to show up at her side. "I just caught a family of thrushes and they posed beautifully."

"Good." Brian nodded and slipped his hands into his pockets. *I saw your twin at La Chantilly last night,* he wanted to say. *Or could it have been you, Sydney? Being entertained by two men...?* But when it came time for the words, they didn't come. The delicate issue of etiquette reared its head. She'd been away—somewhere—on business. Her business, not his. He couldn't ask her where she'd been, because he didn't have any right to know.

"You look tired."

She nodded. "Business makes me tired. But I had a good day yesterday." She smiled and then looked off toward the stream, examining its surface and its meandering route carefully for further subjects.

"Well, that's great, Sydney."

"For me, not you." She smiled honestly and let the camera rest against her breasts for a moment. "I'm starting to get some money, Brian. You need to know that."

"You have the million dollars?"

"Well, no—" she laughed throatily "—not all of it. Not by a long shot, in fact. But the response has been good. And I do intend to get the rest."

Brian lifted one leg and rested it on a slanted rung of the fence. "Why are you telling me this?"

She shrugged. "I don't know exactly, except I think you should know. In case you need to plan on another deal, or whatever it is you do when something doesn't work out for you."

"Sydney, things usually do work out for me," he said quietly.

Sydney didn't answer. She continued to click her camera and Brian concentrated on her, not loans and winning, and found it far more rewarding. He watched her snap a single woodchuck as it sat back and stared at them from across the stream before hopping back into the tangle of bushes and undergrowth. "Do you suppose he's like the aborigines who fear you steal part of them away when you take their pictures?"

"I don't think so. I think he's a natural ham and will probably return for another pose." Sydney shifted against the fence and angled her body sideways, rotating the lens around until it focused on Brian. "And what about you, Brian?" She clicked the camera several times before it occurred to him what she was doing.

"Hey." He laughed, lifting his hands up in front of him.

Sydney snapped once more, then lowered the camera and smiled teasingly. "Well, how do *you* feel about being photographed? As brave as my woodchuck? Or do you think I've stolen part of you away?" The question had been innocent and in fun, an effort to move as far away from their business talk as she could get. But the words came out soft and throaty, not at all as she'd intended.

Brian's eyes had darkened. "That's easy," he said. "I *know* a part of me has been stolen. But it's okay; you don't have to give it back."

Sydney wet her bottom lip and played with the camera. It was difficult to maintain eye contact with anything as active as Brian's eyes were at that moment.

"You hide behind your camera, I think," Brian said.

Sydney looked across the creek and followed an imaginary line along the edge of the trees. "I don't."

"Not ever?"

"I don't think so. I don't think I hide from things, Brian. I'm a pretty up-front person."

"If that's the case, why, in the short time we've known each other, have our conversations centered on me?"

"Maybe you're more interesting or a better talker." Sydney laughed and snapped a squirrel that had stopped for lunch beside the water.

Brian held back a smile. Her camera *was* protection, whether she admitted it or not. And she used it very effectively. "That's doubtful. And I know there are things about you I'd find fascinating. Things I'd like to know more about." His fingers lifted her hair off her neck, and he watched the silky strands slide like honey through his fingers. "Personal things—"

Sydney shivered and her camera clicked again.

"—like how your hair got to be thirty-four different colors. Sydney and the hair of many colors. Someone should take a picture of *that*."

Sydney let the camera fall and turned toward him, her face soft with smiles. "Well, it wasn't Clairol."

"I didn't think so. You would have had to buy too many bottles."

She nodded as she picked up her pack and slipped her camera lens inside. "I used to hate my hair. Kids teased me about being a bottle babe when I was little."

"And you probably aimed your camera at them and fired."

Sydney laughed easily. She and Brian started down the path that led to the inn. "No, I told them it was the latest thing in Paris fashion and if they had any sense they'd follow suit."

"Did they?" His arm looped comfortably around her waist.

"Oh, yes. Much to the principal's chagrin. And mine. And my mother's and father's. You see, I helped them, and we soon had a classroom full of oranges and blues and a lovely purple shade."

Out of the corner of his eye, Brian could see a mischievous sparkle in her eyes that reminded him of a mythical wood nymph. Or a full-grown Tinker Bell. Sweetly sexy and full of surprises. "And your parents, were they terribly upset when you got in trouble?"

"They were always stern faced and scolding in front of the people in charge, but each one found private delight, I think, in my antics. I don't know—" Sydney's voice grew softer "—maybe they should have been more strict."

"I think you turned out just fine."

"I was spoiled in a very odd way. Overloved, you might say."

"That's a strange claim."

She lifted her chin slightly as she walked, enough to catch the warmth from the fading sunlight. Brian watched the easy tilt to her head and the way her face spoke before her words came out.

"Maybe it's silly; I don't know," she said quietly. "My parents aren't your ordinary run-of-the-mill, folks-next-door kind of parents."

"No." His fingers applied slight pressure to her waist. "I wouldn't have expected ordinary. Parents of a Sydney Spencer Hanover would be unique. How did you get all those names, anyway? It's quite a load for such a delicate body."

Sydney shoved her hands in her pockets but left his arm looped around her waist. Its comfortable pressure made her feel as if she could lean backward freely without a qualm. Brian's arm would catch her. "Well, the Spencer is my mother's, the Hanover my father's."

"And the *Sydney*?"

"You want the truth?"

Brian nodded. "I can handle it."

A tiny smile creased her face. "I was conceived in an old inn in Sydney, Australia."

Brian's husky laugh reached out and touched the air around them. "Thank God they didn't make a stop on the Galápagos islands."

"Oh, I don't know, it has kind of a nice ring to it."

"Nope. *Galápagos* is much too wide a word. Now *Sydney*, on the other hand, has a lean sensuality to it that's entirely appropriate. Besides, who can spell Galápagos?" Brian picked a bright red blossom off a wild-looking bush and tucked it snugly into Sydney's hair. "Was Sydney a special place for them?"

"Nope. But they ran out of money along about Australia. Someone befriended them and gave them a place to stay for a few days. My parents have never met a stranger in their lives. The world seems to open its arms to them."

"Their daughter seems to have followed in their footsteps. I don't notice people closing any doors on you. And I for one would gladly open my arms to you. You just say the word—"

"Okay." She looked at him sideways, mischief lighting her eyes. "Are you good for six hundred thou?"

He grimaced, then grinned back. "Touché. I was thinking more along the lines of those best things in life that are free."

"Ah, one of those conditional givers, huh?" She tossed her head lightly and laughed, and the easy banter strung a fine web between them as they walked back to the inn.

"By the way, why did you come looking for me today? Did you need something?"

"You," he said simply. "I found myself missing you yesterday. I wanted to be with you. And I still do." He watched her to catch her response. Her face was still tilted back, a small smile lifting her lips, and her eyes were thoughtful. The only telltale response was the light blush across her cheeks.

"I think I was more comfortable discussing intimate secrets, like my name." Besides, Sydney thought, she wasn't at all sure she believed him. There was still the inn, always the inn, there between them. He was a businessman, and it was his business to get it.

Brian reached out to hold open the inn's screen door. "Okay, I'll discuss anything you want—the weather, migrating geese, pig futures, sex, apple pie—you name it."

Sydney laughed. "In spite of everything, Brian Hennesy, you're a nice guy. Even if you don't always make much sense."

"I'll make all sorts of sense if you give me a chance."

They stepped from the porch into the brighter light of the inn lobby, and Brian noticed her blush was deeper this time.

"Brian, you—"

"Darling!" A breeze like a small tornado whirled between them, cutting off her words, and Brian pressed against the wall. When the motion stopped, he saw that he and Sydney were now standing apart, separated by a gorgeous, otherworldly looking creature with hair the color of ripe wheat and a figure that dancers would die for. She was lovely, dressed in a strange but exotic silk shirt and pants, with a long sash in mauves and blues and greens tied loosely around her minuscule waist. Her hair was twisted and looped around her head.

Brian watched, intrigued, as the woman wrapped Sydney in a swirl of silk and kissed her warmly on the cheek.

Sydney was still as the Statue of Liberty, her expression pleased but calm, her arms wrapping naturally around the lovely creature and pulling her close. When air and distance separated them once again, Sydney smiled warmly.

"Hello, Mother."

Six

―――――

"Darling, darling, always so calm. Aren't you the tiniest bit surprised to see me?"

"You said you might be coming."

"Well, it doesn't matter. All that matters is that you look wonderful. Doesn't she?" She looked over at Brian for the first time.

He swallowed his surprise quickly. "She certainly does."

"Are you one of Sydney's friends?" She eyed Brian more carefully now, her wide hazel eyes scanning him from head to toe. "Now I see. You must be the Brian Hennesy Gus told me about."

She said it with such knowing that Brian laughed. "You're right on both counts."

"And this is Alana Spencer, Brian," Sydney said. She added quickly, "My mother."

"Yes, so you said." Brian shook Alana's hand. Never in a thousand years would he have chosen this woman to be Sydney's mother. For starters, she didn't look old enough to have a child Sydney's age—or even a teenager, for that matter. The eyes were similar, but there was nothing else that would have tied them together. Alana was effervescent, startling. They were both beautiful women, but in such opposite ways that Brian found himself staring first at one, then at the other.

"I'm sorry," he said at last, shaking his head in apology. "Forgive me for being so rude, it's simply that—"

"It's okay, Brian." Sydney laughed. "People do it all the time. Mother and I are a mismatched pair. But we love each other in spite of it." Sydney wrapped her arm around her mother's tiny waist.

"Or maybe because of it," Alana said on a silvery laugh. "We're dear friends, too. Now tell me about you, Brian."

Brian suspected there was very little to tell—that Alana Spencer had pumped Gus for any detail that connected him to her daughter's life. But before he could answer, Sydney spoke.

"Brian is my watchdog, Mother."

"Quaint! Are you a Doberman, Mr. Hennesy?"

"St. Bernard, I suspect," Sydney said, straight-faced. "He's tough but I don't think he's vicious."

"Lovable," said Brian. "St. Bernards are lovable."

"Yes, I should say," Alana said, smiling. "And I don't think it's all bad to be looking out for Sydney. She's very self-reliant, but there are times when she could use some watching."

"I agree," Brian said solemnly.

"Oh, he's not *that* kind of a watchdog, Mother. He's more the spy kind. He hangs around me to make sure I'm not getting the edge on him in a business deal."

"Actually, I'm versatile," Brian said, throwing the ball back. If she wanted to convince herself he was hanging around to spy on her, that was all right. It wasn't the reason, though. His sleepless night had convinced him of that. Business never made him feel this way. And he had ruled out the small Vermont town, nice as it was. It was simply Sydney. And her power was strengthening every day. He had rushed around looking for her today as if a twenty-million-dollar deal depended on it. But all that depended on it in the end was the way he felt when he'd spotted her with that camera hanging around her neck and the soft, golden smile she'd sent his way. But he'd play along with her game for a while and take this slow and easy. Hell, he didn't really understand it himself.

"Business—oh, I see," said Alana, sounding slightly disappointed. "Well, I can't think about things like that on an empty stomach. And mine is getting ready to roar, darlings."

"My thoughts exactly," Brian said graciously. "May I have the pleasure of taking you and Sydney and Hortense to dinner tonight?"

Alana lifted one hand to Brian's shoulder and smiled brilliantly at him. "That, my dear St. Bernard, would be lovely. As long as it's soon."

"How about eating right here at the inn? Okay with you, Sydney?"

She shook her head. "I promised Gus I would take some photographs of the *Oktoberfest* tonight. He wants them as a memento. Besides, I think the dining room will be closed, since the kitchen crew helps out at the picnic."

"An *Oktoberfest* in Vermont?" Brian lifted one brow.

"It's a New England version," Sydney explained. "They bring lobsters and clams and crab instead of bratwurst, but there's plenty of beer. It's fun."

"I remember now," Alana said. "It's quaint. We shall all go!"

"Do you mind?" Brian touched Sydney's cheek.

The connection, the light rub of his fingers on her face, seemed separate from everything else. It was so sensual and caring that it forced Sydney to take in a long breath before she trusted her voice. She slipped her camera bag onto her shoulder, then looked steadily at Brian. "Your expertise as a camera assistant is a little questionable, but if you stick to cracking crab, I think it'll be okay. And Grams would love it.''

The shared memory of Candlewick Pond floated somewhere in the background, and Brian held Sydney's gaze as long as he could, then followed her with his eyes as she linked her arm through her mother's and walked out the door, taking another inch of him with her.

They all met at the inn and walked the short distance to the small park at the center of town. Brian took Grams's arm and told her how lovely she looked. Then he held out his other arm and Alana obligingly slipped hers through, her flowered dress swirling gaily about her as she walked. Sydney followed a short distance behind with Gus and Ellie, chatting about the kind of photos they wanted and wondering if Sam Bartlett would still be up in the bandbox with his mandolin after having triple bypass surgery, and whether or not old Mrs. Gentry's strawberry muffins would last through the first hour.

Sam *was* on the bandstand strumming his mandolin, right alongside other lifelong residents playing accordions, the string bass and clarinets. And the strawberry muffins were hidden somewhere in a sea of white tablecloths that displayed prizewinning pies and cakes and dozens of rich-smelling covered dishes. The grassy area was tented by shade trees and hanging Japanese lanterns, and wild flowers spilled out of cracked jugs and planters along the pathways. Chatting people intoxicated by the smell of huge pots of lobster and clams and crabs mingled in the twilight. They were all drinking beer from large paper cups and tapping toes to the medley of tunes coming from the gazebolike bandstand.

"This is great," Brian said, his hands in his pockets, his eyes taking in everything from Josie Friedman's purple hat with the giant, jaunty sunflower on top, to the teenagers collecting in awkward, gangly groups on the sidelines. They seemed determined to put as much distance as possible between themselves and the adults.

"Do you like it?" Sydney asked, coming up alongside him.

"Yeah, I guess I do like it. Surprised?"

"Yes and no." She snapped a picture of a lanky boy leaning against the trunk of a tree and a dark-haired girl shadowed in the stretch of his arm. "Mostly I don't understand it, that's all. I wish I did."

"You mean the usual." Brian watched her as her fingers adjusted the lens.

She nodded. She was tired of bringing it up, but things so black-and-white in her head had a habit of slipping out. Now she was sorry she had.

Brian's voice was weary of the issue, but he answered honestly. "It's business, Sydney. The way of the world. I wish now I weren't involved in it, because it's causing complications I sure as hell never anticipated. But I am involved. It's a job."

He didn't touch her but looked at her with a longing that left her feeling completely scooped out.

"Let's eat. I'm suddenly starving," she said.

Gus had claimed an empty picnic table beneath a spreading maple tree and collected cups of beer for everyone, even Alana who usually restricted her intake to champagne. He and Ellie had also filled the table with baskets of biscuits and platters of lobster, clams and crab. Giant red-and-white checked napkins were tucked unceremoniously into shirtfronts, and when Alana announced that she would die without immediate nourishment, everyone dug in.

"This is pretty close to heaven." Brian leaned forward and filled his plate with more clams. He sighed as he dipped a clam into the bucket of butter in the middle of the table.

Gus nodded and hammered open a crab leg for Ellie. "Ellie and I have decided we'll be back for this next year."

"Smart idea," Brian agreed. "Maybe I'll come back, too."

Sydney looked up with a start, then slowly lowered her head and asked Grams to pass the coleslaw.

The conversation stopped for a moment, but Alana stepped into the silence quickly. "Gus and Ellie, it will be sad to leave Greenbriar, but Phoenix is lovely."

Ellie smiled pleasantly and Gus nodded. "And we've got a great apartment picked out there. Even has a swimming pool, can you imagine? But Gus will dearly miss his work, that's the only drawback," Ellie said. "That and our friends, of course. And Candlewick itself."

"Well, I hear that my adventurous daughter is going to attempt a takeover." Alana looked at Sydney directly, then shrugged her delicate shoulders. "I can't imagine quite why she'd want to do that, but Sydney was never one to do the ordinary."

"And that, dear Mother, is purely a matter of genetics."

"Oh, Sydney," Alana scoffed. "I never tried to buy an inn."

Sydney didn't answer but instead focused her attention on the navy-blue ridge circling the heavy paper plate. Her mother may not have bought an inn, but there was nothing else in her life to tag it as ordinary. Sydney had been there; she ought to know.

Brian watched Sydney carefully, trying to read the memories that played across her face. He could see the open affection for her mother, but there was something else there that was puzzling. And it made him want to protect Sydney. From what, he had no idea.

Alana seemed to adore her daughter, yet there was something in the way they danced around each other's words that was uncomfortable. Grams kept discreetly quiet. He tried to recollect the few things Sydney had told him about her parents, but came up short of an explanation.

"Will you be staying long?" Brian asked at last.

Alana shook her head prettily. "No, Brian, I never settle too long in any one spot. Sydney and my mother can tell

you. Life is far too interesting to become entangled in roots.
I shall leave in the morning.''

He looked at Sydney. She was examining the cuff of her
blouse with unusual attention. He wondered if the rootless
philosophy was one Sydney also embraced, but from the
look in her hazel eyes when they lifted, he seriously doubted
it.

''Mother is a child of the world'' was all she said.

Alana waved away the words. ''And you, Brian; as I understand it, you're a financial genius of sorts who goes
around buying inns.''

''Actually this is my first real inn, Alana.''

''And he hasn't bought it yet,'' Sydney cut in.

''Oh, yes, of course. I forgot. This is all quite a convo-
luted business war, isn't it? But it's nice you're such friendly
adversaries.'' She turned toward Sydney, who was concentrating now on a giant slice of apple pie that Ellie had set in
front of her. ''Sydney, darling, where are you intending to
get all this money for your inn? Heavens knows I don't have
it. Nor your father, I shouldn't think.''

Sydney lifted her thick gold-tipped lashes and smiled en-
igmatically. ''Trade secret, Mother.''

Alana laughed deliciously as if this were some wonderful
parlor game being played between Brian and Sydney. ''Ah,
I see. Well, I've always taught you to be resourceful, darling. May it not fail you now. It would be lovely to have
Candlewick Inn in the family, I suppose. Although it does
have that reputation as a special place for honeymoons—
dating back to Grams's time.... Still, a lovely place to visit.''

Sydney watched her mother with a mixture of affection
and irritation. Everything was such an adventure for her,
such a marvelous game. But nothing was of permanence.
Auntie Mame, her friends used to call Alana. When this
adventure began to wear thin, she'd simply find a more intriguing one, that was all. Sydney had lived with that all her
life. But the frightening thing was that she was finding herself doing the same thing. She'd worked on three different

magazine staffs after college, dabbled in this and that during her engagement to Stanley until she broke that off, then the photography job and now buying an inn. She wondered vaguely whether there was something in one's blood that determined you this drastically and made you powerless to change. She drained her glass, and for a long time she watched Alana.

No, she decided at last. She wasn't Alana. But a sudden wave of sadness swept over her as she realized that the insight didn't solve anything at all.

"I thought last year was my final time to be out there making a spectacle of myself," Grams was saying to the group as Sydney tuned back in, "but I've promised Brian one dance. Shall we, dear boy?"

Brian was standing behind the bench, and he carefully helped her up. Then, holding her gently, he swept her lightly out onto the patch of street that had been cleared for the dancers.

Sydney watched through her camera, snapping shots of the crowd and the musicians, then coming back to the tall, dark-headed man who towered over the diminutive lady in his arms. They swept around the street to the rhythm of an old show tune, and the light in Grams's eyes seemed to light up the makeshift dance floor.

Well, Sydney thought, even if he might be screwing up the balance of her own life right now, it was almost worth it to see Grams like this.

Hours later, Sydney and Brian finally slipped away from the group. Alana and Grams were going home to visit since Alana was leaving in the morning, and Gus and Ellie were off, arm in arm, chattering with their lifetime collection of friends.

"One dance?" Brian asked, pulling Sydney into his arms. The musicians had returned from a break and were daringly trying out a new arrangement of "Blue Moon." "I think I can handle this."

"Brian, I'm beginning to think there is little you can't handle."

"We'll see," he murmured, and led her out to the street.

They moved about the pavement easily, their bodies pressed together and a soothing silence settling between them. Sydney leaned her head against his chest and thought how naturally their bodies moved as one. She hadn't danced much lately, but with Brian it seemed not awkward or new but as if they'd danced together all their lives.

"Your mother is quite a lady," he said presently.

She nodded, rubbing her cheek against the smooth fabric of his cotton sweater.

"I imagine life with someone like Alana was so dull, you probably ran away at thirteen to join a circus."

Sydney's laugh was loose and from deep in her throat. It vibrated against his chest. "How did you know? Trapeze with a little bit of bareback riding thrown in."

"You would have been a great hit in those cute little duds they wear." He pulled her closer, savoring the ease in her body. She'd forgotten somewhere during the course of the evening that she didn't trust him, and it delighted him far beyond reasonable limits. "Alana's a pleasure. And beautiful."

"Yes, she is all that." Their bodies rubbed easily together, and the silence returned as they forgot briefly about Alana and Grams and the world and moved to the slow strains of the music. Brian's fingers spread across the flat lower part of her back, and when he moved them or pressed her closer, Sydney felt it straight through to the front of her body. But that didn't compare to the feeling of his body's unyielding hardness when she melted tight against him. Sydney was floating on Brian Hennesy's tender, sensual charm, and she didn't want it to stop. In the background she could hear the clear sounds of Ernie Devon's clarinet, and she could smell the flowers and the scent of Brian. It was a lovely dream.

When it was over, Brian wasn't ready to let her go. "I need to work off the ten pounds of crab I ate. How about a walk?"

Sydney's mind was wrapped up in far more sensual ways to work off calories, but she said a walk sounded fine and welcomed the cool night breeze that steadied her legs. "It's been a full day. Something simple like a walk will be nice."

Brian looped one arm around her shoulder and guided her beyond the bandstand to where the park stretched into the woods and narrow paths meandered like streams. Beyond the tangled branches of the trees above them the sky was velvety black. A thin orange moon hung near the treetops.

"Does your mother breeze into your life like this often?"

"Mother's unpredictable. One never knows."

Alana Spencer had set Brian back. He'd felt he was getting to know Sydney, but now he wasn't sure, and he was hungry for more intimacies about her life. "Tell me about your father, Sydney. Is he a good match for Alana?"

Sydney thought hard about Dick Hanover. "I guess he's a match for her. I don't know. They managed to design their lives so that it never came to that."

"How do you do that?"

Sydney shrugged, and Brian watched the bright moonlight fall on her slender shoulders. "I only know how *they* did it. They were in love but had this notion that marriage was a fatal blow to wonderful, free relationships like theirs. It was passé, so to speak."

"They never married?"

"No. That's why the Spencer and Hanover in my name. They each tossed in one. It was probably just as well they never married. They were in love for a while. We were a family, oddly enough. But I don't think they have that kind of relationship any longer. They will always be friends, but quite honestly I can't imagine them living together. Not in a permanent way."

"How did children fit into that philosophy?"

Sydney smiled softly at the concern in his voice. "Oh, Brian, I fit in just fine. They treated me like a princess. Adored me. And both of them came from families that had lofty ties back to the colonists, though most of the esteemed ancestors seemed to have lost their fortunes somewhere between the Old and New Worlds. Anyway, I had cousins and all the rest. And although money was always an elusive commodity, I was somehow sent to the best schools just like all the Hanovers and Spencers, and I never really wanted for anything."

"Did the three of you live together?"

"Not officially. They each had an apartment on opposite sides of Central Park. Often we were together in one or the other, all three of us, in this kind of whirlwind adventurous life. I had probably seen more of New York City by my fourth birthday than Ed Koch has today. I went everywhere with them, and they went *everywhere*."

Brian noticed that her voice had risen somewhere along the way as she talked about her childhood. It had become higher, almost like that of an adolescent defending things close to her. "Was that kind of life ever hard on you?"

"Of course not. I had the best of both worlds. Twice as much attention, twice as many presents—"

"I only meant with your friends," he said gently. "Sometimes kids can be rough when one's family is a little out of the ordinary."

Sydney nodded. "I suppose. But I simply convinced them I lived in a fairyland of adventure. They all loved my folks. And they came around sooner or later." She looked up through the crisscrossing branches to the sky.

"You rough 'em up?" he teased, sensing her reticence to pursue the topic any further.

"You do what you have to do, bub."

She tried to look tough, but the delicate, lovely angles of her face were incapable of real hardness, and the effort made Brian laugh.

They reached a spot where the path divided, and Brian looked at Sydney, lifting his brows. She shrugged and he led her to the right, along a rooted path that twisted and turned and slanted downward.

"Funny to have a park like this in the middle of town."

"Oh, I don't know. New York has Central Park; St. Louis, Forest Park; Chicago—"

"Okay, you win. Greenbriar is right up there with all the other famous cities of the world."

He dropped a kiss into her hair, and Sydney felt it sink deep down until it reached the edge of her heart.

"Where does the park go?" he asked.

"It follows the creek, and the creek goes everywhere. If we keep going this way, we'll end up, among other places, behind Grams's."

"Then we can't get lost, so let's follow the moon for a while."

Sydney rubbed her head against his shoulder. "It beats chasing fire engines."

There was laughter in her voice, but she made no effort to stop him, so Brian hugged her closer into the curve of his body and walked on. "You sound like you know something."

"Me?" she teased, feeling the weight of the day float away on the crisp breeze. "What would I know?"

"Mmm." He looked over and touched the tip of her nose with his finger. "You know, we business moguls have ways of knowing exactly what a person's thinking and plotting."

"Oh, you do, do you?" Sydney looked up, then blushed at the possibility. Her thoughts were as mixed as the night noises, but certain ones stood out—the ones that centered squarely on Brian and made the blood in her veins race and her heart swell like a balloon. And they definitely weren't thoughts she could share. Her breathing grew shallow. "I think, Mr. Hennesy, that's a ruse. My thoughts are private property."

He traced her cheekbone with his finger, enjoying the coolness of her skin. "Well, there are no thoughts like private thoughts to arouse a man's curiosity." But Brian knew as he spoke that it wasn't just his curiosity Sydney was arousing.

Sydney slipped her hands into the deep pockets of her skirt and looked off into the thick darkness around them, adeptly changing the subject. "We're going downhill; did you know that?"

Brian's deep laugh was unnerving. "That's okay. Uphill, downhill, no matter. This has been a roller-coaster ride from the start."

"What has?" Sydney asked the question before she thought better of it.

"Our . . . becoming friends."

A knotted root beneath her feet sent Sydney tumbling forward, but Brian's reflexes were finely tuned. As his fingers tightened around her shoulder, his other arm moved quickly in front of her, breaking her fall. With gentle movements he pulled her steady against his chest. "See what I mean?" he whispered. "You're falling for me. Twice now."

"And you're as corny as Kansas," she breathed into his clean-smelling cotton.

"But lovable." He put his hands on her shoulders and moved her an inch away, just enough to look down into her face. The sliver of moonlight that lighted her eyes seemed to have found a permanent home in the large hazel ovals. Brian's breath caught in his throat. "Maybe just a little lovable?"

"In a peculiar way." Sydney wondered if he had heard her; her words were muted in her own ears by the hammering of her heart. The power of it, the sudden power of her desire, seemed to be pounding at her from the inside, trying to get out.

"Good," he murmured. "Peculiar is all right." His fingers wove through the feathery tangles of her hair and tugged her head back until her face was just beneath his and there wasn't any other place for her to look.

He wasn't expecting the sensuous smile that tilted her lips and flowed from her eyes. He didn't know quite what he was expecting. At that moment all he knew was that if he didn't kiss Sydney again—soon—he'd probably lose a vital life function. "Sydney—"

She slipped a finger up to his lips. "Shhhh. Sometimes, Brian Hennesy, you have a tendency to talk too much."

"I do?"

Her answer came on tiptoe, a gentle crush against his lips that filled him with a desire squeezing him inside. He felt ready to explode.

"Oh, Sydney," he murmured against her lips, then closed the tiny space again, hungrily exploring every tiny part of that lovely mouth he'd remembered and tasted over and over again in his mind. He wanted to slow down, remember everything. The feelings Sydney tugged out of him weren't to be rushed. But every gentle movement of her body, every touch of her fingers winding into his hair was setting off tiny, incredible explosions inside him.

Footsteps and giggles tore them apart.

Brian tugged Sydney over to the edge of the narrow path. "Company," he growled, the taste of Sydney still reeling inside him.

"Hey, man—" A young man's voice floated across the way. "What's doin'?"

He was sixteen or so, and wound around him was a giggling blonde with messed-up hair, smeared lipstick and a dreamy smile on her face.

Sydney ducked into Brian's shadow. It was Gus's nephew Jimmy.

"Lots of room down there," the teenager said as he passed, his eyes now on the low dip of his friend's blouse. "Have fun!"

"What's going on?" Brian asked, tipping Sydney's chin up.

"Probably plenty, considering the picnic and all," Sydney said. She slipped her arm through his and pulled him along the path for a short distance until it stopped abruptly, shooting off to the right and the left. Straight ahead was the slow-moving stream. And to the right, downstream a hundred more yards, was a rustic wooden bridge outlined against the moon.

Brian and Sydney stood silently for a few minutes, adjusting to the brighter light in the clearing, and it was then that the shapes appeared. Positioned about the moonlit clearing in the private turns of the stream and standing together like pretzels on the old footbridge were shadowed forms of teenage couples. Around them the crisp air moved with muted sounds of nature: the crickets, the wind in the forest and a medley of husky, drawn-out squeals and gasps and shy laughter.

Brian stared at the sight, the movements of young passion gently rocking the landscape as hands and arms, gleaming as they passed through moonlight, wrapped around shoulders and groped for hidden treasures. "Lovers' Leap," Brian said quietly.

"They call it Makeout Marsh here," Sydney whispered, pressing into the warm curve of his body. "It's not really a marsh, but someone liked the alliteration, I guess. Care to explain your motives in leading me down this beaten path, Mr. Hennesy?"

Brian's quiet laughter folded around them. "Seems to me you're the one who knew where we were headed."

A couple near the stream turned and walked slowly toward them. As they brushed passed Brian and Sydney, they peered at them for a moment in the darkness. And then soft, bubbly laughter erupted. "Way to go, man," a shaggy youth said.

"Enjoy!" his black-haired girlfriend whispered.

"Even without our wheelchairs?" Brian looked down at Sydney.

"I think we'd better head back before someone becomes really concerned and calls Med Act."

"We could match any one of them." Brian kissed the top of her head and turned with her toward the path.

"Two of them," Sydney corrected. She slipped her arm around his waist and matched his long loose-legged stride. "Is there any time when that place isn't so crowded?"

"Why?"

"I want to go back with you and neck on the bridge."

Another swaying couple passed them.

"Brian Hennesy, I'm surprised at you!" she said when they were out of earshot.

Brian cuddled her to him and dropped tiny kisses on her ear. They'd reached the picnic clearing, and Gus and Ellie stood a few feet away with a group of friends, but it didn't matter. "No, you're not," he said.

Sydney was silent. She wasn't surprised, of course. Their minds were on the same wavelength, traveling along the same dream.

But the band was still playing, people were milling about and drinking beer. The world hadn't changed during their walk.

Sydney sighed. "I have time for a few more pictures for Gus, Brian, and then I need to see my mother and to get some sleep."

Brian held her for one more minute and she didn't object. She stood there quietly pressed against him. He wasn't going to rush this and scare her off—he'd promised himself that. He'd give her space. But he'd be there when it was time for the space to close, come hell or high water . . . or a million dollars.

Seven

———

Two days later Sydney walked through the doors of Candlewick Inn and found Gus and Brian seated at the round oak table in the corner. The entire tabletop was covered with sheets of yellow paper, and their concentration was so thorough that they didn't hear her come in.

"Brian, you're a hell of a genius," Gus was saying.

Sydney stood silently by the door for a minute, watching the two of them. Gus's narrow gray head nodded solemnly as Brian scribbled across the papers, punching down his pencil here and there for emphasis. Brian's face was serious but full of excitement as he talked. A shaft of dark hair nearly covered one eye, and the effect on Sydney was startling.

She bit down hard on her bottom lip and walked across the braided rug toward them.

"Hi, you two. You look awfully serious."

Brian looked up and slipped his pencil behind one ear. His flashing dark eyes focused directly on her face and revealed more than words could how he felt about seeing her. And the penetrating desire in his gaze set off in an instant the peculiar fleet of butterflies inside her. She felt like those kids at Makeout Marsh, with hormones going berserk at the slightest provocation. Except there wasn't much that was *slight* about Brian Hennesy. And she was far from being a kid.

He stood and pulled out a chair. "Hey, Sydney, join us. Gus and I are just having a little fun over investment strategies."

"The guy's a marvel, Sydney. You should have him teach you some of this stuff!" Gus's eyes were bright. "We're planning my retirement, putting all the dollars in the right holes, and Brian thinks maybe I should invest in a small cabin here for my return trips. He found one yesterday over near Talbot's—"

"Found you a cabin?" The muscles around her mouth tightened. No, she didn't want her feelings to flip-flop. That had happened so many times since she had met Brian Hennesy that she was beginning to feel like a chameleon.

"It'll pay for itself, and I never would have thought of it!" Gus said.

"Gus, what are you talking about?" Sydney carefully avoided Brian's eyes. She breathed deeply. Damn! He had her emotions so messed up she could hardly separate defiance from desire.

"I'll rent it out while Ellie and I are gone, but we'll always have a place to come back to—"

Brian saw the tightness in her face but decided to ignore it. Instead he said calmly, "The rent around here will cover his mortgage plus some, and he'll have the appreciation as an investment when he finally does sell it. It's a great deal."

"Is this a conscience salve?" she asked abruptly.

Brian walked over to her and touched her shoulder. His voice was firm. "No, Sydney. It's a friend helping a friend."

Sydney tried not to look into his eyes because she lost control when she did. Damn this man. "You're taking away the inn and giving him a pacifier."

The phone rang then and Gus looking relieved, slipped away into his office.

"Sydney." Brian raked his hands roughly through his hair, then took a long breath and released it very slowly. He looked at her steadily. "I'm getting tired of this. Every time you and I move an inch closer, you manage to pull this inn thing up to hide behind. You're *using* it, Sydney, and I don't know why."

"I'm not."

"You are." His voice grew harsh, and Sydney looked up, startled at the intensity behind his words. "And it's foolish. You're a bright, sensitive woman, so I know you don't believe those things that come out of your mouth. This is *business*, and sure, I like Gus; I even like this inn, for God's sake!" He looked around, suddenly aware that his voice was attracting attention from the nearby dining room. He grasped her arm and pulled her out onto the screened-in porch. "But face it, Sydney. It's probably going to go to the Goodlin company because you don't have nearly enough money yet, and not a lot of time left, but that shouldn't—"

"How do you know that?" Sydney's eyes grew cold and she tried unsuccessfully to shake free of his grasp.

"I know that because Grams told me. She's concerned about it. And she thought maybe I could help."

"Grams," Sydney sputtered. "She wanted *you* to help?"

"Yes," he said, his voice softening slightly. "And the damnedest thing is, I would if I could, because then you wouldn't have anything to hide behind, and you'd let whatever this is between us take its natural course. Maybe. Maybe you'd find something else to hide behind."

"You're crazy, you know that?" Her head began to ache.

"Maybe a little. Crazy about you. And you have feelings about me, too, dammit, but you're afraid, Sydney. And I'm not sure what you're afraid of, so I don't know how to help."

"I'm not afraid of anything. Who do you think you are, coming in here and disturbing everyone's life, messing—"

"Stop it, Sydney. You're not being fair."

Sydney's heart pounded in her ears. What had happened to the bright, sunny morning she was enjoying a half hour ago? And the delicious feeling she had had when she spotted Brian in the inn? She thought of herself as a strong, capable woman, not one to crumble like a dry cookie whenever the wind changed direction. With a violent shove, she managed to free herself from his grasp and stormed out the side door of the porch, the wooden frame banging clumsily behind her.

"I'm not through!" Brian shouted. The door slammed a second time and he was beside her, his fingers wrapped tightly around her arms and his broad chest blocking her from moving an inch.

"There's one more thing, Sydney." His voice had dropped from anger to a husky, ragged sound that frightened Sydney far more.

She looked up, fighting back the tears that were threatening to spring from the total confusion squeezing her heart. "I think you've said enough, Brian."

His eyes were dark with a passion so stormy that it stopped her breath. She didn't have the strength to protest or the steadiness of reason to fight him. Her whole body went still.

The shadow of his head bending, angling over her, and the black storm of his eyes were all she saw before she closed her eyes.

The press of his kiss was grinding and fierce. The room spun around, but Brian was holding her so tightly there was no chance of her falling. His lips continued in relentless possession, his tongue tracing the gentle curve of her lips, then plundering within until her knees were weak and the hands she'd raised to his chest when he'd grabbed her trembled over his thudding heart.

Abruptly he set her away from him and looked darkly into her eyes.

"Now I'm through," he said quietly. In one smooth movement he turned and walked into the inn.

For five days Sydney tasted his kiss on her lips. That must be some kind of a record, she thought vaguely as she worked through a stack of letters.

She threw herself headfirst into the week's work, convinced it would impose some reason on her irrational behavior. Brian made no attempt to see her, and that was just fine. Any man who could cause her to act so impetuously couldn't be good for her.

She put every ounce of unspent energy and highly charged emotion to good use, calling dozens of acquaintances, following leads, writing letters and contacting friends. She'd had a brainstorm as she watched the sun lift from the hills one morning, and it was making an enormous difference in her finances for the inn: time-sharing.

The inn had a whole wing of spacious bedrooms with small sitting rooms attached that would be perfect for it. And there'd be other rooms left for drop-in, overnight guests. She'd run it past her lawyer, then burned the phone lines convincing friends that buying a share in Candlewick Inn and having a getaway place when pressures in the city became too great was simply the thing to do.

By the end of the week, she had promises and confirmation letters equaling nearly seventy percent of her goal. She'd show Brian Hennesy a thing or two about business!

"Well, Grams," she said on Friday, "we're making progress."

"That's grand, sweetie," Grams said happily, looking as if a burden had been lifted from her thin shoulders. They were having lunch together on the screened-in porch off the back of Gram's house. "Now why is it that you're not glowing with that news?"

"I'm pleased, Grams."

"But looking like something the cat dragged in. No offense, Asparagus." She glanced over at the pitch-black cat with piercing green eyes who occupied a wicker chair in the corner. Then she concentrated on Sydney's pale face. "Lands, Sydney, the light in your eyes is flickering out."

Sydney mustered a short laugh. "I'm tired, that's all." Tired of the whole thing. Tired of being on the other side of the fence from Brian, tired of pretending she didn't care about him, tired of waking up thinking of him, tired of wondering if he'd ever kiss her again. The list was as endless as the nights had been.

Soon this whole thing would be over—this inn mess. That's what she needed most of all: a return to normalcy. But the remembrance of Brian's kiss made her want that least of all, even while she wanted it most of all, because at the end of it there would be no reason for him to stay.

She rose from the chair and began stacking the luncheon plates.

Grams watched her through pale eyes. "What will you do next, Sydney?"

Sydney's mind pulled the question apart, and she smiled at her own craziness. What was next? Giving in to the swell of emotion and attacking Brian Hennesy in the inn lobby? Having a brief fling and satisfying her carnal appetite? Doing the dishes? Taking a walk?

"Actually what's next, Grams, is the Phipps Gallery party tomorrow night?"

"You are certainly pulling out all the stops, Sydney, dear." Grams knew well Sydney's dislike of New York society galas. It matched her own, which was why she'd chosen long ago to live in the quiet hills away from all that.

"For Candlewick Inn I'll go to the Phipps extravaganza."

"Who will you go with, dear?"

"I'm going alone," she said softly.

"Oh, Sydney." Grams sounded so sad, Sydney couldn't suppress a smile. "It's all right, Grams. I could go with Stan or someone, I suppose, but I'm going to the party to work the crowd. I can't do that if I have a date."

Grams sipped her sherry, the frown beginning to lift. "Dear Sydney, you sound like a gun moll. 'Working the crowd'—goodness." But her eyes sparkled with the adventure of it all, and Sydney knew that if she could, the lovable aging adventurer would be right there beside her.

"All those people I haven't been able to reach will come out of the woodwork for the Phipps, Grams. And you know how generous they get at these events, especially with everyone looking on. . . ."

"Sydney, you're becoming devious."

Sydney grinned, feeling the cloud begin to lift from her shoulders. "Just directed."

"Too directed, sometimes," Grams said vaguely, her mood shifting nearly as drastically as Sydney's had these past days. "Don't miss the forest for the trees, sweet pea."

"Grams, you lost me." Sydney swept the crumbs from the table into her cupped hand and picked up the dishes, her thoughts moving ahead to the weekend plans.

"There's more to life than buying inns, you know," Grams said with a thoughtful smile.

Sydney tossed her head. "I know that, Grams. There's a contract to fill for *Vermont Today*, and a whole life to move ahead with."

"And there's Brian Hennesy," Grams slipped in when Sydney turned toward the kitchen.

She stopped in the doorway, balancing the plates in her hands. "No, Grams, I don't think there is."

"You're attracted to him."

"Sure. More than that, maybe. But we're too different, and I don't think I'm much more than a diversion for him. I don't know, Grams. It just doesn't seem to be a match made in heaven." Sydney forced a bright smile to her face. "Now, dear one, would you like some pudding? And then I have to leave."

"Pudding shmudding. And whoever led you to believe matches were made in heaven?" Grams lifted herself from the chair and headed for the outside door. "Matches are made right here on good old Earth, right in the midst of war and peace and political messes." She looked confused for a minute, then added quickly, "And sometimes auctions."

Sydney's breath came out in a burst of laughter. "You think so, do you?"

"Young lady, I know so. Didn't I meet your grandfather in a haggle over land? I won and he was the

cream on top." She threw her head back haughtily.
"So there. And now I'm going to go to the barn and
settle this thing once and for all. Maybe once the inn
is taken care of, you can see through all those cobwebs you're spinning in your pretty head."

And before Sydney could point out that she wasn't
looking for a match at all, Grams disappeared down
the path to the barn. It wouldn't have mattered anyway, she knew. It was a Spencer trait not to listen too
carefully to others once your mind was made up.

Sydney stood there for a long time, watching the
shadows of the maple trees play across the meandering path. A trip to the barn seemed to solve all
Grams's problems these days. Maybe she should start
spending some time out there.

She sighed and walked slowly inside to finish up the
dishes.

The Phipps Gallery was housed in a spacious, ele-
gant town house on the west side of the park, and on
Saturday evening its three stories were ablaze with
New York society.

Sydney mingled in the entryway and considered
looking for a phone. She should put Grams's fears to
rest and let her know she was not alone. Sarah Mur-
ray Levin, her old Radcliffe roommate, had been on
the reception committee for the gathering. When
Sydney had finally called in her acceptance the day
before, Sarah had insisted that she join the Levin
party, and Sydney had accepted.

She had spent more time than usual dressing for the
evening. And the final selection, a strapless sea-green
gown that hugged her breasts and hips then swirled
gracefully to her ankles, was a perfect choice. It was
elegant and lovely, and she knew it emphasized her
best physical assets. And that was fine, she'd decided
as she brushed her hair into a loose ripple of waves

about her bare shoulders. No sense in skimping on the ammunition when it might help the cause.

When Sarah and her husband picked her up for the party, Sarah's gasp and David Levin's open stare gave her the final vote of confidence she needed to attack the evening with all her wits intact.

And then she discovered the Levins' party of several couples also included one unaccompanied male. And he was all but wrapped up in bows and handed to Sydney. "Hank had a rough divorce, Sydney. He just needs a friend—" Sarah had whispered as they walked past the tuxedoed butler.

When the party of eight sat down together at a round table skirting the first-floor dance floor, Sydney realized what kind of a friend Hank needed. His hand landed on her thigh almost before she was seated, and it returned there like a well-trained homing pigeon after each gracious brush-off.

"You're just what the doctor ordered, Sydney," he said, his eyes hungrily devouring the cleavage visible in the dip of the silky gown.

"Oh, you don't look very sick to me," Sydney murmured as she peeled his fingers from her knee.

Later, when Hank went to greet an old friend, Sydney quickly excused herself and fled up the thickly carpeted stairs to the upper level. For the gala event, the second floor had been transformed into a lavish gambling casino, and she looked in on a sea of smiling faces gathered around the croupiers' tables, eagerly losing money to benefit the arts.

Sydney smiled into the gaiety. This was much better. She'd lost Hank and could finally start to work. The rooms were lighted with lamps hanging over the tables, and it was difficult to make out familiar faces, but within a short time she had successfully cornered two old acquaintances who were now potential timesharers in Candlewick Inn. Sydney's spirits lifted with each group she joined. She was making definite progress, and she hadn't thought about Brian Hennesy more than seven or eight times. Maybe by the time she returned to Greenbriar tomorrow she wouldn't be thinking of him at all. Or at least not with such unnerving intensity.

It was that intensity that frightened her. He'd become a *presence* to her; she could *feel* him when she thought about him. Her body responded to the thoughts, her pulse quickened, her mind grew less clear. It was all very disturbing. Sydney accepted a glass of champagne from a passing waiter and smiled away her discomfort. Now was the time to find money for the inn, not worry about Brian. She took a sip of the champagne and forced her full attention back to a friend of her father's who was admitting it might be very nice to take the family to an inn now and then.

From his seat on one side of the room with his back to the dice and gambling, Brian Hennesy looked into the eyes of a lovely blue-eyed brunette—and thought of Sydney Hanover.

The whole thing had reached totally improper proportions, Brian told himself. Sydney had inched herself inside him and resided there as certainly as his heartbeat. He hadn't invited her, hadn't planned on this. But it had *happened*, that was certain.

"We thought you had given up socializing altogether, Brian. It's been a long time since I've seen you."

Brian pulled his attention back to the room and the husky voice at his elbow. He chided himself, then smiled at Marian Plesir. "I've been out of town, Marian. On business."

Business? No, that wasn't it at all. It was Sydney. She might not have been why he landed in Greenbriar, but she sure as hell was why he stayed. And now it was because of Sydney that he was *in* town. When he'd finally gone to her grandmother's, she was gone. Business for the weekend, was all Hortense Spencer said, although it was obvious she wanted to say more. But this business was Sydney's private world. He didn't belong in it now, and she sure as hell didn't want him there. And with Sydney gone his excuses to Jim Goodlin lost their luster, and he'd agreed to attend the annual Phipps Gallery event.

"Well, I must say, Brian, business out of town agrees with you." Marian fingered the lapel of his tuxedo and smiled warmly. "I've never seen you looking better."

It was true, Brian thought honestly—at least if he looked the way he felt. Greenbriar and Candlewick Inn had been a magic tonic for him. Greenbriar and Candlewick Inn and Sydney.

"Brian has become an innkeeper," Jim Goodlin said from Marian's left. "He's keeping our inn safe and sound."

Brian cringed involuntarily, but he managed to keep a smile in place.

"Brian the innkeeper." Marian laughed, and her words lingered in the air between them.

Brian looked out the windows behind her and into the blackness beyond. The lights from the city flickered, but he didn't see them. *Brian the innkeeper*. It had a certain magical sound to it. He smiled at the incongruity of it all. Brian the innkeeper. Keeper of Sydney's inn ...

"What do you say we go downstairs and dance awhile?" Jim suggested to his wife and the other couple, and Brian's thoughts disappeared into the distraction of chairs moving and bodies rising.

He took Marian's arm and began to weave her through the mass of festive people crowding the gambling tables. And then it happened again. A body moved, his eyes lifted, and the woman with the hair of many colors, the Sydney look-alike, appeared across the room. She was standing at an angle, her profile just visible through the smoky air, and she was talking animatedly to an older man who hung on her every word. He could see her better this time, the gorgeous curves of her body defined sensuously in a dress the color of deep ocean water. She was enchanting, a creature of the sea, a...a *Sydney* in the guise of a goddess. The air thinned and he took a long breath to steady himself. It was absolutely uncanny. Without thinking, he began walking toward the far side of the room.

"Brian?" It was Marian who stopped him, her hand on his arm and her eyes searching his face.

Jim Goodlin looked at Brian and recognized the hazy look. "Oh, no, Brian, not again. I think you need to have a doc check you out. One drink shouldn't put you in another world like this."

Brian focused on the group around him and cleared his head. "Sorry, folks, I just thought I saw someone I knew—" He looked toward the corner, but all he saw was an elderly couple trying to get away from the press of the crowd. He scanned the room. No flowing green gown, no slender goddess.

With the faint thought that maybe he *should* see a doctor, Brian followed the others out of the room.

Sydney was elated. The night had been a tremendous success. She felt more and more confident that Candlewick Inn might truly escape the hatchet. She wasn't there yet, but she was certainly closer.

Voices called out to her as she drifted past, and she smiled hello. It was only when she found Sarah and her husband at the downstairs dessert table that she realized what an emotional strain the evening had been. She had put her heart and soul into getting funds for Candlewick, but it would never be tops on her list of how to spend a month. The effort had left her exhausted.

"Sarah, I think I'm going to sneak out early—"

"Sydney! We haven't had nearly enough time to catch up, and Hank will be distraught! Where have you been, anyway?" Sarah motioned for her to sit, but Sydney held her own.

"There were so many people I needed to see, Sarah. You understand. Please make my apologies to Hank, and thanks to both of you." She brushed kisses across David and Sarah's cheeks and turned to go, but she was one minute too late.

Hank had spotted her from the bar and was weaving his way to the table. "Sydney," he said sluggishly.

"Oh, dear," Sarah murmured. "Since he didn't have you, Hank found a bottle to keep him company."

Sydney watched him approach and braced herself. "Hank, I'm glad you're here. I have to leave, you see, so th—"

"Leave? But the night is young, and we've only begun to get to know each other!"

His eyes were half-closed, and Sydney wondered how he even knew who she was. "It *is* a shame, Hank, but maybe some other time—" Sydney pulled out the chair so Hank would have a place to land and started toward the door.

But cool partings were not what Hank had in mind. Before Sydney could stop him, he had wrapped her in his arms and swept her back in a dramatic arch. And with the Levins and several dozen party goers watching, he proceeded to bid her farewell in a manner reminiscent of Scarlett and Rhett. As Sydney finally slipped out of his hot, alcohol-smelling embrace, Hank succumbed to the chair and tipped an imaginary hat at her.

"It's been swell, Hank," she muttered, reaching for the lacy shawl that had slipped to the floor in the fracas.

From the patio doorway, Brian watched idly as the huddle of people on the opposite side of the room parted for the man with the unsteady walk. He smiled in mild amusement as the man scooped a woman into his arms and swept her back into a Fred Astaire hold.

And then his heart stopped.

It was the mystery woman again, and with her head tilted back and her fine cheekbones flushed with embarrassment, Brian would have sworn it was Sydney.

The kiss lighted the smoldering fire beneath his feet, and he headed off across the room.

Sydney, dreading an encore, hurried out the doorway and down to the street. "Taxi!" she called, wrapping the thin shawl about her shoulders. "Oh, dear, where are you fellows when I need you!" She looked up and down the street and moaned. Not a cab in sight.

She looked around at the brightly lighted street, glanced at her watch and made the decision. It was a beautiful night and her apartment was only a short distance away. Hugging the shawl closer, she waved to the doorman and set off down the street.

Brian caught just enough of a glimpse to know it was the right woman. Her dress lifted on a breeze and fanned behind her in a hazy green cloud. And by the light of the streetlamps he could see the burnished sheen of her hair. It was she, whomever she was. This was crazy, but he had to see where she was going, had to prove to himself it *wasn't* Sydney. It couldn't be; she was on business, Grams had said, and the meeting would last late into the night.

Then who was she? Sydney's twin? Or maybe he was so bewitched by her at this point that he was seeing mirages. He almost feared he'd get up close, reach to tap her politely on the shoulder and his fingers would poke only air.

The thought of the gorgeous woman being made of air made him smile, and he quickened his stride, slowing down only when the distance between them was a few yards. He didn't want to scare her, just get her off his mind. And he wanted to know for sure that the kiss he'd seen was between strangers.

The image plagued him, and as foolish as it was, he couldn't shake it. He'd see where she was going, figure out who she was, then go home and go to bed. And maybe get a good night's sleep.

The woman ahead slowed down briefly to look in the window of a small gallery.

Brian stopped in front of a pet store and pretended interest in a cage of snakes. He tried to see her out of the corner of his eye, but a cascade of shimmering hair hid her face from view. All that appeared was an enchanting medley of shadows.

Brian waited a few seconds after she started up again, then fell in step behind her, the shadows weaving eerily across the sidewalk. As he passed the gallery that had held her attention, he glanced at the window. It was a photography exhibit. He quickened his step.

Somewhere along the fourth block, the crisp night breeze began to work on Brian. Slowly the realization of what he was doing inched into his consciousness. "Acting with half a brain," he muttered to a slumped figure leaning against a dark building. Adolescent foolishness at its best. He'd always prided himself on seeing his way clearly and succinctly through business mazes. And here he was at midnight, following a phantom Sydney.

He began to walk faster. He'd simply stop her, satisfy his irrational curiosity, then apologize and be done with it. Sleuthing belonged in movies.

Just as Brian moved close enough to approach her, the woman took a turn at the corner. He spun around the corner after her. "Excuse me, miss," he said, one hand extending in front of him.

Before the words had time to register, Sydney went into action. She gulped back the fear that had been terrorizing her for three blocks, stopped dead in her tracks as she'd been taught, then spun slightly to her right.

Before a sound was uttered, she had hooked her right arm beneath his left, arched her body forward and rolled the six-foot-three figure over her back and onto the dark sidewalk.

Eight

For a brief moment there was a macabre silence. Sydney's breath was labored, her heartbeat the only sound that stirred the air.

She stared down at the man in front of her. He was on his side, his body still, his face bathed in purply shadows, and her shawl was matted in a lacy puddle beneath him.

As she filled her lungs with huge gulps of the night air, the fear around her heart began to ease its painful hold. Slowly it softened, then spread into manageable shreds, and her mind began functioning again on a rational level.

And then her eyes began to put the shadowed pile of man into perspective.

"Oh, Lord, it can't be—" Her hands flew to her face, and she fell to her knees beside the still form.

Brian opened one eye and strained to level his head. If the figure leaning over him would stop spinning around, maybe he'd be able to make sense out of this.

"Oh, Brian," Sydney said softly, her hands cradling his face.

The voice was foggy but familiar. Maybe he was dead and it was someone from another life. No, he couldn't be dead, because there were no clouds or bugles or wings. His mind seemed to be working. A dubious sort of progress, he thought, but something.

The other eye pulled open. Behind the angel hovering over him was a light. It turned her hair into a fiery mass of waves. Nice . . .

"What in damnation were you doing?" Sydney cried, silently begging him to sit up or talk or swear or raise hell.

The voice was sad and furious at once, Brian thought vaguely. Interesting . . .

"Brian, speak!"

The angel pressed her hands against his cheeks, her face coming closer. The sweet perfume of her body reached down and tantalized him. Magically both eyes began to focus. Her features slowly aligned themselves, the three noses converging into one and the lovely form quieting.

Brian took a long breath and released it slowly. Against the black night illuminated by a nearby streetlight, everything became clear. His head hurt, but it didn't seem to matter much anymore. "Hi. It's you."

"Yes, it's me," she whispered roughly. "You were expecting Elizabeth Taylor, maybe?" Her hands touched a long jagged scratch on his cheek.

Brian winced. "Nah, she'd never be this much fun."

"What in the name of heaven were you doing?"

"If I have any memory left at all," he said slowly, "I didn't actually do much. A neat little flying act, maybe, but you did most of the work." He tried to smile but his lips didn't work easily.

"Brian, you were following me! You scared me to death. Don't *ever* do that again."

"Sydney, you have my word. But before we get into all this, I have a small request—" He grimaced with discomfort.

"You only get one," she said softly, her eyes avoiding the darkening blotches on his face.

"Could we find somewhere a little more comfortable to talk? Maybe a nice asphalt driveway or even a stretch of mud—"

Her soft laugh was coated with concern. She slipped one arm beneath his head and cupped his elbow with the other. "Can you get up?"

"Not as quickly as I got down, but in good time. How the hell did you know how to do that?"

Sydney rose to her feet and gently pulled on his arm to help him up. "Brown belt in judo. That was a basic throw. I've never had to use it before—"

"Well, congratulations." Brian let her wrap one of his arms over her shoulder and leaned slightly into her side. "You're pretty good."

"It needs some work. If I had done it correctly, you'd have landed flat on your back, not on your side." She looked up at him and smiled. "Want me to show you?"

"Maybe later, Wonder Woman." He walked slowly beside her, their bodies pressed together for support.

"Turn here." Sydney nudged him toward a short flight of cement steps.

"Where are we going?"

"My apartment."

Apartment? Brian's head began to fuzz again, but he suspected it was a combination of things this time, the assault to his mind as well as his body. There was so much he didn't know about this lovely lady who had taken over his senses. The people she hung around with. An apartment in New York. For maybe the first time in his life he'd let his soul get all involved before his mind sorted out the facts. "You ... don't mind taking me in at this hour?"

Sydney looked at his disheveled tux and the bruises deepening on his face like a developing image on film. "You look pretty harmless, Hennesy. Besides, the least I can do is clean you up.

Her apartment was on the second floor, and they made it there slowly and carefully, Brian relying heavily on Sydney's support. Even through the aches and pains, the contact with her was wonderful.

Sydney unlocked a door at the top of the stairs and helped him through. A flick of the switch on the wall bathed the medium-sized room in soft light. "Here it is. Home sweet home, at least occasionally."

She helped Brian move to an oversize couch at one end of the room, tugged off his torn jacket and bow tie and settled him down on the cushions.

"That feels good," he said, laying his head back on the soft pillows she positioned beneath him.

"Be back in a minute." She disappeared through a door to the right, returning with a glass of water and two pills. "Take these, Brian. They'll help you over the rough spots."

Brian didn't argue; he could feel the stiffness settling into his joints, and his head hurt like hell. Propping himself up on one elbow, he swallowed the pills and fell back into the couch.

"Now, let's see what's under all that." Sydney inched herself onto the small space left on the couch and with a wet cloth began gently cleaning the bruises on his face. "Doesn't look too serious."

"You think I'll pull through, then?"

"Almost sure of it—" she smiled softly "—but you're going to be very colorful in the morning. Does it hurt?"

He tried to smile. "Mostly my pride."

"Are you ready to explain why you followed me like that? And in a tuxedo! New York has a lot of strange people in it, but I've never heard of a masher who wears a tux."

"I always do," he said, his eyes half closing.

"The truth, Brian." She winced as she carefully washed away the dirt and tiny pebbles embedded in his skin.

"All right, that's fair I guess. I saw someone at the Phipps Gallery tonight who looked like you, except she didn't wear jeans and carry a camera. She was dressed like a beautiful sea nymph—" He fingered the silky foam of her dress as he talked. "It was you, and not you—and when a man swept the beautiful sea creature off her feet and kissed her, I had to make sure it wasn't you." His fingers played with a pleat at her waist and his voice dropped. "But it *was* you."

Sydney laughed softly. "But he didn't exactly sweep me off my feet."

"Who was he?"

"No one to me," she said simply.

The relief he felt came as no surprise. "I think I also saw you at La Chantilly a few days ago. Same man?"

She shook her head and placed a cool cloth across his forehead. "That was a business meeting with two good friends. One is married to a friend of mine, the other I used to date, but he has happily gone on to other fish in the sea."

Brian watched the soft light in the background fall across her bare shoulders. They glowed with a creamy translucence. "I see," he said slowly.

"Why didn't you just ask me? Or approach me at the party?" She stroked his wrist softly as she talked.

Brian felt the caresses with startling clarity beneath the hazy sheen of the medicine. "When I saw you at La Chantilly, I still wasn't sure it was you. I didn't fit you into places like that, and I guess my mind had trouble with it."

"I see. And the Phipps?"

"That was more of the same. Also, we've both tried hard to keep things separate, and Hortense said you were away on business—the none-of-my-business side of you."

"Actually the Phipps was business, too, in a way. I don't usually go to those things."

"You seemed right at home. So at home I didn't think it was you." His fingers played across her arm. "When I think

about you, which is quite a bit these days, I think about a
beautiful woman with a camera about her neck. Someone
who finds beauty in old fences and woodchucks and the
flight of birds. Someone whose body looks lovely dressed in
worn jeans, her hair tossed by the wind—'' His eyes fell to
the daringly low dip of her dress, and the words stopped
short.

Sydney heard the catch in his voice and felt the drop of his
eyes to her breasts. "Well, sometimes even we country girls
need to dress up."

"You look ravishing, Sydney." His voice was husky, and
the words were coming out more slowly now.

"It was all part of a greater plan," she joked, trying to
laugh away the blush creeping down her chest. "Why were
you there?"

"It's one of those things we business people do. Con-
tacts. Perhaps you understand that better than I know." He
narrowed his eyes, but Sydney only smiled.

"Actually, I wouldn't have gone," Brian continued
slowly, "except you disappeared from Greenbriar, along
with my good reason to stay there. So I came in to check my
office, and Jim Goodlin coerced me into attending the
party." He tried to climb back into his mind and figure out
the evening. Right now the sequence of events was foggy
and faraway. He wondered briefly if he had said goodbye to
the Goodlins. *Or* to Marian Plesir. But the thoughts were
too difficult to deal with, and he concentrated on Sydney.

"Well, I guess that's reasonable," she said. He seemed to
have forgotten the stormy scene when last they'd been together. She hadn't forgotten it, but somehow in memory it
only fueled her desire. The anger she remembered had been
passionate anger. Not reasonable nor rational, but a side
product of the way Brian made her feel. "Did you...did you
enjoy the party?"

A frown collected between his brows in reply, and Sydney smiled. She was trying not to move beside him, not
wanting to pressure any part of him that was bruised. But

his hand had crawled silently into her lap and the sensations it created with each movement made it increasingly difficult to sit still and keep her end of the conversation. "Are you . . . are you feeling better, Brian?"

He rolled his head back and forth across the pillow.

"What?"

"My head," he pointed in the vague direction of the pillow.

"What should I do?" She smoothed her hand very lightly across his cheek, knowing in a secret part of her what she'd like to do. His eyes were closed now, and Sydney openly traced the strong lines of his cheekbones, the dark shadow on his chin. The roughness of it tingled her fingers. She wet her lips and released her breath slowly and steadily.

Brian stirred, his lids still closed. "I think it might help if . . ."

His voice drifted off and Sydney bent closer to hear. "What, Brian?"

"I think it'd help if you kissed it—"

Her lips eased into a smile as she watched him point to one of the bruises. "Really? You don't think I'd hurt it?"

"It'd be . . . the best medicine in the world."

Gingerly, with hands braced on either side of his body, Sydney leaned down and brushed a kiss next to his finger.

"Better?" she murmured, lifting her head just far enough to look into his eyes.

They opened halfway, far enough for Sydney to see the light flickering in the blackness. "Much."

"Where else?"

His finger moved to another spot on his cheek. "Here."

Sydney followed his finger, then kissed the purply spot gently.

"And here—" he traced a line on the other side of his face.

Sydney shifted, and with the slight movement her breasts brushed the front of his shirt. When she glanced down, she saw with a start what Brian was seeing. Her dress had pulled lower when she had helped him up the stairs, and now the soft green edge just barely covered her nipples. The rest was flushed, bare skin.

Brian followed her gaze. "Beautiful," he said sluggishly. "Just like all of you. You know, Sydney . . ." His voice fell off.

"Know what?" Sydney watched the play of emotion wash across his face.

"You've made me shift, darlin'—"

"Shift?" She lifted his hair with her fingertips, pushing it gently from his forehead.

"Shift my thinking, my pace of living, priorities, that sort of thing." His eyes had closed again, but his arms circled her body and locked her next to him, pulled closely to his side. "Didn't see it at first, but you have."

She wasn't sure what he was talking about. Or if he even meant or knew what he said. But sitting there against him, quietly relishing the feel of his body, was enough for now. Without thinking, she laid her head gently against his chest.

Brian's hand lifted and his fingers combed through her hair in slow motion. "My darling," he murmured.

Everything inside her shifted into a new gear. Her breathing grew labored and her heartbeats were quick and insistent, almost painfully battering against her chest. Tiny flames of desire licked at her from inside.

"Oh, Brian, what are you doing to me?" she whispered into his chest.

When his fingers slowed, then finally stopped their soothing movement through her hair, she lifted her head.

His hand had dropped down beside him, and his chest rose and fell in a gentle rhythm. His mouth curved in the beginnings of a smile. He was sound asleep.

Sydney sat there for a long time, first calming her feelings to a manageable level, then watching him sleep.

His face assumed a peacefulness she had caught glimpses of over the past weeks. It had come at odd times—when she'd walk up to meet him in front of the inn and find him looking off toward the rise of Green Mountain, or the day they'd gone looking for picture frames for some of the photographs of hers that he'd bought in local galleries. He had enough now, she had teased him, to wallpaper his room at the inn. But he had wanted frames, and he liked Sydney's idea of old ones found in tiny secondhand stores. So they'd set out and spent the whole day from late morning until sunset scouring the countryside and laughing together in a lovely, careless way.

Brian had completely unwound that day. Sydney had found it contagious, and when he'd kissed her good-night it had been with a new gentleness and understanding, but also with a passion that was becoming increasingly difficult to control.

They had frightened her, the enormous feelings that Brian's kisses pulled to the surface, and she had tried to douse them by reminding herself why he was there, and that he'd soon be off on some other business deal. But it was becoming more and more difficult, and resorting to adolescent anger wasn't diminishing the intense feelings at all. She'd let him sleep the night there on the sofa, and maybe tomorrow she and Brian could have a talk, get things straight. Even though she hadn't the faintest idea what *straight* would be. She knew only one thing; she couldn't be a one-night stand or have an extended love affair, no matter how she felt about him. She couldn't live the uncommitted life her parents had laid out for her to see.

He moved slightly then, and Sydney watched an expression flicker across his face. Was he dreaming, she wondered? And if so, she wondered what Brian would dream about. Part of her was trying to read it in the lines across his face, and another part shied away. Dreams were private, and sometimes it was better not to know. It was beginning to matter too much what Brian cared and dreamed and hoped for.

Her hand slid gently across his chest until it was stopped by the round, smooth buttons on his shirt. Slowly, carefully, she unbuttoned them and spread his shirt apart. It was too much of a task to remove it, but she could free him a little from the restraint and make him more comfortable. Moving off the couch, she looked down at the long legs and tugged off the shiny black shoes. His feet stuck over the edge of the couch awkwardly. Sydney smiled.

"Sleep well, my darling," she whispered, smoothing a quilt over his quiet form. For a long moment she stood over him, watching him sleep. Then slowly and without a second thought, she leaned down and kissed him good-night.

The soft gray light of morning filtered in across the hardwood floor, and Brian stirred in the stillness. The strangeness of his surroundings seeped in and tugged his eyes all the way open. Slowly he looked across the room, taking in as much as he could see without moving his head. For a brief moment he had no idea where he was.

And then he lifted his fingers to a rough patch on his face and winced. The past hours fell into bold focus: the party, the flying arc he'd taken over Sydney's shoulder, the apartment.

Her apartment. He looked carefully around the room. It was washed clean with stripes of sunshine that fell through the blinds. There was very little furniture, and the walls and ceilings were all a soft gray with white trim, but color was pulled into the comfortable room through the pictures that hung on the walls and the bright pillows and area rugs on the dark wooden floor. It was beautiful, carefully put together and without any frills. A simple beauty—like Sydney.

She entered his thoughts and vision at the same time. Directly across from him, curled into a ball on two chairs that had been pushed together, Sydney slept. Her hair was loose and free, falling over her face in soft, sweet innocence. She looked seventeen years old.

Brian's heart lurched, and another sensation followed immediately: the familiar tightening in his loins. How had he managed to get through last night, he wondered, with her so close and his feelings swollen to dizzying dimensions. His dreams had run swiftly and unrestrictedly through every fantasy he'd tried to quiet the past month. He'd made wonderful, sweet love to Sydney Hanover, and she'd responded to him with every lovely fiber of her body.

When he tried to lift himself from the couch to see her better, the reality of the night before hit home in a far less romantic way. He moaned as stiffness held him fast to the couch.

Sydney didn't move.

Brian shifted himself about more slowly until he was sitting crookedly with his back pressed into the couch and his view of Sydney was more aligned.

She had traded the lovely evening gown for a white T-shirt with letters across the front, and a plaid stadium blanket was pulled carelessly over her. Her bare feet stuck out from beneath the edge, perfect delicate arches and slender ankles. She must have raised the window a narrow slat before going to bed, because the morning breeze lapped at the edge of the blanket, lifting it in slow graceful movements from her sleeping form.

The scene was not extraordinary, but it touched Brian in that way. With deliberate slowness he eased his body from the couch and walked gingerly across the polished floor. The movement put some confidence back into his body, and the stiffness seemed to lift slightly. A floorboard squeaked beneath his weight, but the only thing that registered on Sydney's face was an unearthly kind of joy. Resting against the chair arm, he watched sleep play across her features and thought of how very much he wanted her.

Like an unconscious extension of his thoughts, his hand slid down and touched her hair. Thick waves fell across her forehead and curled against her cheek prettily, and reddish-gold strands lay in the shadowed hollow of her collarbone. The blanket had slipped down to her waist, and her breasts rose and fell above it in the gentle rhythm of her sleep. Peace. Quiet. The eye of the hurricane, Brian thought with a smile, fighting the arousal that just the sight of her stirred in him.

He could see the pink nipples clearly beneath the thin shirt and had to curl his fingers tightly into his palms to keep them still. What incredible power a sleeping woman can have, he thought. Pulling gently on the large T-shirt, he smoothed the folds enough to reveal the script-printed letters.

Are We Having Fun Yet? he read.

"Beginning to, my darlin'" he whispered.

Sydney stirred and the movement filtered into his thoughts. "Good morning, Sleeping Beauty," he said.

She pulled her eyes open and a slow smile lifted her lips. Amazing, she thought hazily. Open or closed, her eyes saw the same thing. She spoke softly with the huskiness of sleep. "Good morning, Brian."

He touched her cheek with the back of his fingers.

"You should have wakened me."

Before he answered he brushed her hair from her cheek with the palm of his hand. Her skin was warm from sleep and softer than the velvety feathers of the ducks she loved. It left a nice feeling on his hand. "Sydney, why are you pretzeled up on these chairs instead of sleeping in the bedroom?"

Amusement laced her sleepy voice when she answered, "This *is* the bedroom, Brian. And the living room and the kitchen. The bath is through that door."

Brian looked around again at the simple, uncluttered apartment, then focused on the wide couch on which he had slept so soundly. "Your bed?"

She nodded. "A Hide-a-Bed. But once you were settled last night, I didn't have the heart to move you again to pull it out."

"So I took your bed?"

"No, I gave you my bed."

"I owe you one, then. Anytime you need a bed, Sydney—"

"Thanks," she said quickly. He was far too close to her and to her dreams to talk about beds. She concentrated instead on his face and the purple areas that looked raw and sore. She lifted one hand and touched the largest one, half covered now by a shock of hair falling over his forehead. "Still sore?"

Brian shrugged, his attention diverted for a moment by the sunlight playing across her tangled hair. "I think I'll soon be ready to face life again."

Sydney watched the playfulness in his deep blue eyes. With his tousled hair and bruises, he looked more like a carefree, devil-may-care youth than a tough businessman. The thought broadened her smile. "Well, not just yet, I hope." She pulled herself upright, and the T-shirt unraveled around the tops of her slender legs. "Breakfast will be served momentarily. This is a first-rate hotel."

With a push of her toes, she separated the two chairs and stood up.

Brian hadn't moved. Her fluid movements, natural and uninhibited beneath the wrinkled T-shirt, were playing with his mind. Breakfast wasn't at all what his body was telling him it needed.

"Why don't you go back there to the couch, Brian, and make yourself comfortable," she said.

Brian breathed deeply and did as he was told, concentrating on the apartment as a distraction. But it didn't work, either. "This place is a lot like you, Sydney."

Sydney followed his gaze. "I like it here well enough. It's tiny, but when I need to stretch, I always have Greenbriar."

He looked at the tastefully framed batiks and the clean photographs on the walls. "It's so uncluttered."

She nodded slowly, moving around in the tiny alcove that served as a kitchen. "I've never really cared to have a lot of *things* around. I used to think of it as something lacking in me—"

"But now?"

"Well now, for the past few months anyway, I see it as liberating." She plugged in the coffeepot and tossed over one shoulder, "And so much easier if one gets the urge to dust."

Liberating. The word flickered across his mind, then settled, blazing, in one spot. That's what Greenbriar was doing for him—pulling him free of the rigid path he had set for himself and allowing him to see sunsets and green fields and the uncomplicated beauty of Sydney Hanover.

He walked to the couch, not even noticing the stiffness of his body. He folded the blanket into a neat square, then sat down on the broad upholstered cushions.

Sydney came to him, carrying two mugs of hot coffee, her bare feet slapping gently against the floor as she walked. "Here, this will wake you up." She sat down next to him, folding her legs beneath her.

For a moment they sat in silence beside each other, with the only sounds the hushed Sunday traffic beyond the window. And then Sydney broke the silence with laughter. Brian's followed immediately.

"We're quite a sight," Sydney managed between her giggles. "Look at you."

Brian shook his head as he looked down the length of himself. His stiff, open shirt was pulled free of the elegant tuxedo pants, and both were patterned with mazes of wrinkles.

"I'm going to look awfully strange parading the streets like this."

Sydney nodded. "You certainly are." And she laughed again, her fingers playing with the stiff points of his shirt. "Maybe we can get you out of this long enough for me to take an iron to it. It might help a little."

She looked up and found Brian's eyes steady on her face. They'd walked around their feelings, ducked beneath the emotions that had been running rampant in the tiny apartment for a night now.

But Brian had stopped the dance with one dark, intense look. It was as lasting and passionate as the most intimate kiss.

Sydney's breath caught in her throat, and the unsteadiness of her pulse caused her to set the mug down on the coffee table.

"Brian, I—"

"Sydney—"

The words collided in the charged air, and Sydney's quick, nervous bubble of laughter followed.

"You go first," she said then, shakily.

Brian was silent for a moment, as if studying his words inside his head. He hadn't felt this ever before, the intense need to make a woman know she was so special, so important, not just a romp. He didn't want to demand things she wasn't ready to give, but he knew clearly and certainly he couldn't let her push many more things between them. He reached out and touched her cheek. His eyes never released her. "Sydney," he began slowly, "You've come to mean a great deal to me."

Sydney's eyes never wavered. She looked at him steadily. "I've been thinking about that."

"It's not just the physical pull, you know."

"I know." She smiled softly. "But I don't know what that means exactly."

"I don't, either," he said raggedly. "And I also don't know how much longer I can stand having you so close to me and not make love with you."

Sydney released the breath that was threatening her early demise.

"I've wanted to for a long time," he continued, "maybe even as long ago as the day at the inn when you burst into the auction—"

The memory seemed a lifetime ago, she thought remembering. Or the beginning of a life, maybe, because Brian had never strayed far from her thoughts after that.

His hand had circled her shoulders and pulled her closer to him. Sydney slipped across the cushions easily and her head fell naturally against his shoulder. Brian rubbed a lock of hair that fell between his fingers. "I don't know if it's witchery or magic, but you do something incredible to me, darlin'."

"Maybe a little of both," she murmured against his chest. "But it's not me. It just *is*." A flicker of fear passed through her briefly. She was frightened at the passion she felt, frightened that she knew she was going to make love with Brian, that she had wanted to for days and that things wouldn't be the same afterward.

"It made me a little crazy when I saw that guy kiss you," Brian was saying into her hair, and she fought to concentrate on his words. "I wanted to grab him by the shoulders and punch out all his lights."

Sydney didn't answer, because her thoughts couldn't focus distinctly on anything at that moment. Brian's hand had dropped into her lap, then moved downward, and now his thumb moved lazily back and forth against her inner thigh.

"I don't remember ever being jealous before," Brian went on, his voice a slow caress. "It's a blinding thing. Unpleasant."

Sydney was quiet against his open shirt, his words stroking her as surely as his hands. The tenderness in his voice seeped deep inside her, and she wanted to bask in it and let him take over completely. She didn't want to make decisions or rationalize or take charge; she wanted to float away on the wonderful buoyancy of his hands and his voice and his breath, so warm and sensuous on the side of her neck.

"I seem to be running over with words here, my love."

Sydney smiled. "You have a nice way with them, Brian." But *she* didn't. Not now. Because if she spoke she would have to tell the truth. And she wasn't ready now, and might never be, to tell Brian that she was falling in love with him.

Brian's hand sliding the T-shirt fabric across the flatness of her belly settled her thoughts and buried her fears. Her feelings were real and right, and she wasn't going to let the future hurt them today. Brian cared for her; that was as real to her as the fires licking at her wildly. For now that would be enough. Her hand reached over and pressed against the hard wall of his chest beneath the open shirt. "We talked about taking this off to iron it—"

"If the heat I feel is real, it's being ironed right on me."

"We can't let that happen." Sydney slipped her hands beneath the white fabric and pushed it over Brian's shoulders and down his arms. "Does it hurt?" she asked, thinking of the soreness of his body.

He smiled dreamily. "Soreness is a state of mind. You took me out of that state a long time ago."

"Perhaps we could bottle this magical cure."

While Sydney folded his shirt and placed it on the coffee table, Brian peeled his undershirt over his head and concentrated fully on the long-legged woman in the T-shirt. "You're the magical cure, my darlin', and there's no way I'd keep you in a bottle." He slipped one arm behind her head and lazily traced the arches of the letters written across the front of her shirt.

"A-R-E," he read slowly, his fingers following the swoops and lifts with tantalizing slowness. The *We* captured one breast completely, and with a sigh Sydney dropped her head against the wide back of the couch. "Oh, Brian, you should write more often."

"I think I have a natural bent for it," he said modestly, his finger moving up and down the *H* in *Having*. He lowered his dark head and kissed the spots left vacant by his fingertips. He could feel the change in her against his lips, the growing tautness of her breasts beneath his touch.

"And now we come to the best part. I never noticed before how many curls there are in a *U*, did you?"

Sydney's head answered slowly, moving back and forth across the soft gray fabric of the couch. Her whole body was spinning wildly about, and she opened her eyes to see if it was the entire room moving or only herself. And at that moment it stilled. Brian's hand stopped, and she turned her head slowly, focusing on his face.

He was watching her, his eyes as dark as midnight. "Well, darlin', are we?" he asked, his fingers beginning to move again and looping sensuously over the question mark on her shirt. "Are we having fun yet, Sydney?"

Sydney felt the caress in his fingers and in his eyes at the same time. "I . . . I don't think that's exactly the best choice of words." Her voice was labored, filled with a thickness that seemed to come up from somewhere deep inside her. "I've had fun before. I've never had this—"

Brian caught the edge of her shirt and lifted it from her skin, moving his fingers along the edge from one shoulder to the other. The shirt was loose and stretched, and he slipped it easily down one shoulder until the pink rise of her breast was visible. His fingers moved slowly back and forth across it, tracing the rise and the faint blue lines that grew more visible as her skin tightened.

The coolness of invading air washed over her skin, and Sydney felt his eyes focus there. Then she felt the brush of his hair against her chin as he dipped his head and trailed his tongue lovingly over the warm, creamy skin. "Oh, Brian," she murmured against his neck.

The magic of his tongue playing on her skin made further talk impossible. He licked circles around her nipple, teasing it, working it, until Sydney thought she couldn't stand it any longer. She dug her fingers into the hair at the nape of his neck and hung on. Her body shivered with delight.

"Cold?" Brian lifted his head.

"Very warm," she answered huskily.

"We can handle that." With adept, strong movements, he straightened up and pushed the T-shirt down over both shoulders, then lower down her arms. "Hmmm," he murmured, stopping briefly as the shirt tightened around her ribs. Her breasts fell free while her arms were held still against her body. "This is a dangerous position, m'lady."

Sydney's eyes smiled brightly and displayed no fear.

He held her captive for a moment longer, his large hand cupping each breast in turn, caressing the pale mounds, his thumb rubbing gently in small circles. "You're very beautiful, my love." He continued down then, pulling gently on the shirt and tugging it lower.

As Sydney lifted her hips, he pulled it completely free of her and dropped it in a puddle on the colorful rug beside the sofa bed. Slowly his eyes traveled up the length of her naked body.

She sat still and unashamed beneath the heat of his gaze. Her eyes never left Brian's face as he explored without touching the smooth planes and shadowed valleys of her.

And then he couldn't stand it any longer, and his hands were on her, smoothing along the silky skin of her legs, caressing her thighs and gliding over the gentle slope where her hips dipped into her abdomen. Sydney reached out and twisted her fingers into the furry thatch of hair on his chest. She teased him closer, pulling a coarse strand with her fingertips, and he dipped his head kissed the thin blue threads inside her wrists.

"I think we need to approach this more evenly," he said, pausing briefly to tug off the rest of his clothes. "There. Now we stand equal. Or sit . . . or lie." He slipped her back on the wide couch and positioned himself alongside her, propping himself up on one elbow. In the thin morning light she looked almost ethereal—long and lovely and untouchable. But she was touchable at last, and Brian felt a surge of joy. He wanted to go slowly, to please Sydney, to bring her to the height of happiness he'd dreamed about.

"When you're not trying to be guarded, you have very expressive eyes, Mr. Hennesy," Sydney said.

Brian lifted one brow while his hand made lazy circles on her navel. "Don't tell my foes that."

"Never. But I know all your secrets."

No, she didn't know them all or she wouldn't be meeting his eyes with such a clear gaze. His secret thoughts would confuse her, puzzle her, just as they did him. No woman had stirred him in quite this way, and he knew Sydney couldn't deal with that right now, even if by some incredible gift from the gods she felt the same. He knew it instinctively, as he knew when to be cautious on a business deal, when he should plunge in with full force and when he should hold back. Slowly, Brian, slowly, he promised himself. And the promise was meant for Sydney, too.

Sydney watched the play of expression across his face. Maybe she didn't know all his secrets, but she knew enough to know the feelings burning inside her were shared completely by this man. She reached out slowly and laid her hand on the flat wall of his belly. It was firm with a band of dark hair that was rough and sensuous to her touch. Her hand rubbed slowly back and forth, and she reveled in the feeling. He was strong and tough on the outside, but beneath it she could feel the warm gentleness inside him. In that way he was different from any man Sydney had ever known, and the combination was so combustible, she felt near-painful arcs of fire pass through her.

"Your hands on me are a pleasure I've dreamed about, Sydney," he whispered as he wrapped his arms around her and pulled her body tight against his. They were perfectly lined up, naked hip against naked hip, her thighs graceful and slender against the iron rock of his thighs, which were shadowed with dark hair. He kissed the hollow of her throat.

"Me, too," she murmured. "That . . . and more."

"X-rated dreams?"

"No, wonderful, life-giving dreams."

"As wonderful as this?" Brian said raggedly as he slid his hand down over the smooth expanse of her belly until his fingers cupped over the mound between her legs. His hands were gentle, adoring, as if it were the first time he had touched anyone so beautiful. She was acutely aware of every nuance, every movement, each caress of his fingers until finally she couldn't hold back the soft moan of pleasure.

In the quiet sunshine he watched the intense pleasure sweep across her face. A thin sheen made her face goddess-like, a smooth carved likeness with a smile so soft and sensual that she would challenge the world of art forever. Brian felt his own surge of desire as he watched her, and he clenched his jaw tightly to restrain the intensity of his feeling.

His fingertips teased and caressed and loved her until she had to bite down hard on her bottom lip and her back arched in response.

"Yes, Brian," she whispered into a stream of sunlight.

His hand slipped to her hip and held it with the flat of his palm.

Sydney waited in rapt and aching expectation, her breath coming in ragged gasps. And then she felt his magnificent body move over her, and there was a warm, smooth sliding inside her. As the sunshine that had lain across their bodies burst into flames about them, Sydney dug her fingers into his back and burrowed her head into his shoulder to quiet the rumble coming from deep in her throat.

Brian felt near explosion, too, his nerve endings hot and painful. The pleasure of being one with her overwhelmed him, and he fought to slow himself down.

"No, Brian, don't. I need you—" The words nearly a cry. Brian found the lips that uttered them, and their tongues tangled in hot, deep kisses. They were fierce and hungry and loving at once, and Sydney felt herself rise above ordinary things.

"I'm doing it at last, Brian," she gasped, her hands moving across the smooth, shifting muscles of his back.

"What, my love?"

"Flying, way above the ground, the treetops—"

"Here's a cloud—" He drove deeper inside her, and they both tensed, their bodies taut and powerful and one.

Sydney felt suspended above the cloud, silent in a world apart. And then the sky lighted up and propelled her up-

ward with unimaginable, fiery force, and Brian's cry met
hers in the vast, explosive space.

For an indeterminate time, thought was suspended as they
lay silently wrapped in each other's arms, legs tangled, their
breathing slowed and their bodies pressed together in the
deepest peace.

When she finally opened her eyes, Brian was looking at
her and his fingers were gently stroking out the tangles of
her hair.

"Glad that cloud was there to catch us," she said softly,
her eyes bright and raw with feeling. She felt strangely and
wonderfully giddy.

"I ordered it just for you." He kissed the tip of her nose.

"What does one do for an encore when something this
wonderful happens?"

"We'll have to explore that issue in good time." He
brushed her lips with a kiss.

She nipped playfully at his finger as it passed by. "I think
you're quite wonderful, Brian. Remarkable."

"Me?" He eased onto his side and lay quietly next to her,
loving the light in her face.

"You. Us. This."

He nodded against her hair, understanding, and dropped
tiny kisses into the hollow of her neck.

She lifted her shoulder into the tickle and basked in the
cradle of his arms. She felt needed and cherished and wonderful. Perhaps she would spend the rest of her life right
here on the broad contour of this couch.

Brian settled into the back of the couch, holding Sydney
in his arms as carefully and delicately as a valuable piece of
porcelain. His body was spent and deliciously filled with the
pleasure she'd brought him. It lingered there, as if she had
left some of herself connected to him, as if he were somehow still within her.

"You're awfully quiet." Sydney pressed her fingertips to
his lips.

"Just enjoying you, that's all," he said, pushing her hair from her face.

"You better watch what you say, mister, or we may be taxing those sore muscles of yours beyond capacity."

"Never," he said, and the tightness began again in his loins.

"I don't think you know your body at this minute as well as I do."

His brows lifted in pleasure at the thought.

Sydney raised herself on one elbow and answered his thoughts with a quick kiss planted on his eyelids. "And my good sense tell me it needs food right now. And rest. At least for a little while." She ran a finger down his chest and circled his navel slowly, a wicked smile appearing. "But only for a little while."

Brian groaned. "You are a witch."

She shrugged playfully and swung her long legs down beside the couch. "Well, let's see then what kind of a brew I can mix up for breakfast." She reached for her T-shirt, but Brian held her arm still before her fingers reached the fabric.

"Don't."

Sydney's brows lifted in a question.

"Please don't put it on. Just for now."

She smiled down at him, surprised a little at her comfortableness with the suggestion. Her body felt beautiful. Glowing. And she rose from the couch with easy grace, nodding. "Okay."

She had never felt this way before, so in touch with all parts of herself. Wholeness, she thought. That's what this feeling was. It was the same way she felt about a photograph when it included all that needed to be there, fitting together perfectly into a single unit.

She brushed her hair with the back of her hand and walked assuredly across the printed throw rugs and the polished hardwood floor. In the tiny kitchen, separated from the rest of the room by a small oak bar and a lush potted plant, she busied herself with eggs and toast and thin slices of honeyed ham a neighbor had brought over the day before. She hummed softly as she worked, aware of Brian's eyes on her but relaxed and at ease.

From across the room, the beauty of her movements affected Brian profoundly. The movement of her high, firm breasts was sensuous and lovely and innocent, all at the same time. She moved with the grace of a child completely at home in her body, unashamed and unaware of the natural beauty.

When she walked to the table to arrange two place mats, the light swing of her hips sent him spiraling again. She was exotic, wonderful and had a power over him he knew he was only beginning to understand.

"Sydney?" he said raggedly.

"Hmm?" She looked over dreamily, and when she turned he caught the full view of her, the rosy nipples of her breasts, the tapered hips, the flatness of her belly and the lovely mound of curling hairs between her graceful legs. And when he pulled his gaze up, her hazel eyes sparkled with challenge. "You called?"

Brian could barely move. He'd explode if he tried to get off the couch. Every part of him responded to her perfectly and painfully, needed her to make him whole. "Say, cook, do you suppose..."

"Yes?" Sydney coaxed, her body standing still and naked, longing coating her voice like thick maple syrup.

"Do you suppose...that is..."

Sydney dropped the silverware on the table. It clanged heavily, but the sound went unnoticed. She walked slowly over to the couch.

Brian saw the naked longing in her eyes. He reached up for her and pulled her down into the warm curve of his body. Her buttocks pressed firmly against the flat wall of his abdomen. When he could speak, his voice was husky and low. "I need you, my darlin'. Do you suppose the eggs can wait?"

"That depends—" She leaned over him and kissed him long and slowly until they both had to pause for air. Sydney's eyes were hazy with need. "And what is it you'd have of me?" she asked throatily.

"I want you to love me," he said slowly.

And she did.

"Things are different now," Sydney said matter-of-factly. They had finished eating breakfast and were sitting on the fat cushions in the window seat, looking down at the street below. A few people walked along the sidewalk, pushing against a brisk fall breeze that sent leaves sailing down and skittering across the pavement.

Sydney hugged her arms around the silk kimono her mother had brought her from Japan, and Brian sat in the freshly ironed tuxedo pants he had worn the night before. Sydney was still flushed from the morning of lovemaking, and Brian couldn't take his eyes off her.

"Yes," he finally said. "You're right. What we had... what we *have*...does change things." He looked at her with clean honesty, and a half smile lifted his lips. "But quite frankly, I don't know what the hell that means."

Sydney shrugged and smiled back. "Me either. Except I feel a great deal more wonderful than I did twenty-four hours ago. Thank you, Brian Hennesy, for that." She reached over and hugged him tightly, then sat back. "And now you need to go."

"Go?" Brian looked at her dumbly.

Sydney touched his cheek with the new familiarity she was already accustomed to. "Yes, my love. You must go. I have to get dressed and meet someone. I'm here on business, remember? And I don't think you'd be an asset."

Business. The real world. Brian tried to feign the look of a cast-off lover, but Sydney kissed the pout away before he could form it correctly.

He stretched, then rose languidly from the couch and turned slowly to her. One finger snaked its way between the folds of the kimono and circled her breast. When she lifted her head to see him, he kissed the long column of her neck.

Sydney shivered.

"Sure you can't cancel your appointment?"

A momentary fear gripped her. No. She drew her brows together painfully to block out the intruding thoughts. That wasn't what this was about. Brian wasn't trying to slow her down on the inn deal. He had made love to her honestly and lovingly, she was certain of that.

But when she walked into the lobby of the Helmsley Palace an hour later to keep her appointment, her body still basking in the pleasure of Brian, a tiny flicker of doubt flawed her new happiness.

Nine

The following days moved along to a new rhythm. It was autumn, and Sydney couldn't remember ever having experienced quite so majestic a season. The hillside colors were blindingly vivid, and she could almost hear the golden leaves falling from the trees. It was a magical sound that stirred her, and when the sun slipped slowly down behind the hills in the west, she sometimes found herself wiping away tears.

"Not smart, Sydney," she said, standing alone in the rolling field behind Grams's house. "How can I take pictures if my vision is blurred?" Asparagus the cat purred agreement against her leg, and Sydney lifted the camera up again, catching a clear silhouette of the old barn against the fiery sunset.

"Sydney?" Grams's voice trailed out from inside the house, and Sydney turned and hurried back.

But it wasn't Grams who met her when she reached the house. It was Brian, standing framed in the doorway, a shock of hair falling loose from the rest, a half smile on his dark face and his eyes lighted with the sparkling blackness that peppered her dreams. He was leaning against the frame, his hands in his pockets, watching her.

By now, she thought, she certainly should have adjusted to the sight of him. They'd stolen hours out of every day this past week, just to be together. But she hadn't adjusted. Her heart lurched, her breathing quickened and thousands of butterflies caused havoc inside her every time she saw him or heard his voice. She was living in the middle of a grand happiness. "Hi," she said softly.

He reached out both arms and drew her to him. "I missed you."

"It's been a long five hours since lunch," she murmured. "I missed you, too."

"Five hours and thirty-two minutes," he whispered into her hair. "Did you get any pictures taken today?"

She nuzzled against the clean-smelling cotton shirt. "Uh-huh. Some."

"Good. Because I brought you a present to celebrate your hard work, and if you hadn't taken any, I'd naturally have to give it to someone else."

"Brian...you shouldn't—"

"Shhh." The directive was followed by a slow, warm kiss that assured its efficacy. He released her, but his eyes still held her fast. "I *do* have to, you see. No matter what you think or say. Because if I weren't finding you things, I'd be following you around all day and you'd *never* get any pictures taken. Or anything else—"

She nodded dreamily as if it made sense. "I see."

"Besides, Grams loves it."

"My present?"

"No, hers. But you'll love yours. Come on." He entwined his fingers with hers, and they walked inside.

Even before she walked into the room, Sydney could feel a presence other than Grams. She looked quickly at Brian, but his face was calm, guiltless, his smile enigmatic. She didn't trust him a bit.

She rounded the corner to the living room, and her eyes focused immediately on Brian's gift. "Brian!"

Grams sat placidly in the hand-carved rocker. And at her knees, pushed up tight against her and looking at her with huge, adoring eyes, sat a grand brown-and-black-and-white St. Bernard.

"Sydney, dear," said Grams, her gray eyes lighted like the fourth of July, "meet Tiny."

In disbelief Sydney looked from the dog to Grams to Brian, and then repeated the cycle once more to see if one part might disappear; the trio remained intact.

"A dog," she murmured.

"*My* dog," Grams said clearly, and Tiny rested his large, floppy jaw on her knees.

"Why?" Sydney looked up at Brian.

He shrugged, a boyish grin lifting his lips. "I always wanted a dog when I was a kid."

"But you're not a kid. And neither is Grams."

"We can pretend, can't we?" He winked at Grams at the same time as his fingers lifted the hair from the nape of Sydney's neck and tickled the delicate skin. Her shoulder moved into his touch.

"Tiny's completely trained in the ways that matter," Brian said. "And he can fetch newspapers, twigs, garbage cans, maybe even groceries and handsome widowers; who knows?"

"And he loves me," Grams said simply as Tiny's huge tongue lapped away at her thin, blue-veined hands.

"He's smart as a whip," Brian added. "He lived with an old man out in the country for a couple of years and did everything for him but peel the vegetables. He's been a mess since the fellow went off to live with relatives."

Sydney looked up at Brian and her heart lurched as the significance of his gift slowly dawned on her. A few days earlier he'd come over to bring Grams some apples and found her in the attic of the garage, unable to manage the steps on the way down. She'd been up there for two hours, he had told Sydney quietly that night. Something needed to be done.

And so he'd found Tiny, the next best thing to a live-in helper, which Grams steadfastly refused to consider.

"I've never much thought about a dog, but Tiny seems to need me," Grams said slowly, "so he can stay, as long as he behaves himself."

"Just like me, huh?" Sydney said softly, her throat tight.

"Yes, sweet pea. Just like you."

Sydney spotted the keg tucked into the folds of Tiny's black-and-brown-and-white fur. She lifted one brow and looked from Brian to Grams.

Grams patted Tiny's head lovingly. Finally she looked up at Sydney and said proudly. "Harvey's Bristol Cream. Brian and Tiny have good taste."

Sydney looked at Brian accusingly. He shrugged. "One never knows when one'll get caught in a snowstorm."

Sydney shook her head, but inside her whole body smiled. He was crazy, but his heart was as big as Green Mountain. "I'm not sure I should mention the other present."

"You probably shouldn't," Brian said. "Who knows what's next? A moose, maybe, or a pair of kangaroos. Give this man a wonderful woman and he goes completely berserk." His arms circled around her from behind, and he squeezed lightly, breathing in the wonderful smell of her that reminded him of crisp leaves and mowed fields and sunshine-cleaned air.

Sydney pressed automatically into the comfortable security of his body, but inside her head the words echoed with a tinny sound. *Give this man a woman...* That's what she'd done, given herself to Brian heart and body and soul. But deep down in the shadowed parts of her where she hid her threads of doubt, she wondered what came after this giving. She and Brian didn't talk about it. It was as if the inn's closing in eight days was a kind of invisible block that they couldn't see beyond. And the biggest fear of all was that there might not be *anything* beyond it.

But that was a thought she couldn't touch right now. Even anticipating what other present he had dreamed up was easier.

"Close your eyes," Brian demanded, and Grams giggled at the drama of it all.

"Grams, you keep an eye on him for me," Sydney said. "Tiny and I will be right here."

Sydney found little consolation in the fact but shut her eyes obediently. She'd trusted him with her heart; she could certainly do this.

"Here." Brian brushed her cheek lightly with a kiss and then slipped a chain around her neck, working the clasp beneath her hair.

Sydney opened her eyes and looked down. From the delicate silver chain hung a rectangle of silver, its surface carved with an unusual pattern. She lifted it into the flat of her hand and brought it closer to determine the design. It was two raised figures, their bodies a smooth series of lines, carefully and artistically carved.

And then her face broke into recognition and she smiled broadly. "Brian!"

"Just a reminder," he said.

"As if I could ever forget."

"A silversmith up near Montpelier made it."

"To order, no doubt."

Brian lifted the medallion from her chest and held it out to catch the light from the lamp. "Well, he said there wasn't much call for stick figures in a judo throw, but if it becomes a fad, he assured me he'd do more."

"That's good to know," Sydney said, fighting a strong urge to smother Brian in passionate kisses right in front of Grams and Tiny. Brian seemed to read her mind.

"Care to go for a quick stroll? You might have time for a couple more photos before night falls."

"Good idea," Grams tossed out. "I need to get busy, and I work far better without you two about."

Sydney looked at her grandmother. "Work? Doing what?"

"Have to finish the attic. Plenty of boxes left in it."

"Grams, what is this? You've been digging around in every closet in this place for days—and the barn, too!"

"Just cleaning, sweet pea. Keeping the house in order." She rose slowly from the rocker, and Tiny looked up at her.

"But you don't seem to be throwing anything out, Grams. You just open and close the boxes and then shove them right back into the same cobwebby spots they came from."

"Waste not, want not," Grams murmured.

"I've an idea, Hortense," Brian said as he leaned over to scratch Tiny's ears. "Instead of cleaning right now, how about if you go up and deck yourself out while I help Sydney with her camera. And later I'll wine and dine you both with the care befitting two such gorgeous women, and when we're stuffed as full as Tiny looks already, I'll come back and pull those boxes down for you."

"A celebration," Grams said happily.

"Sure," Brian agreed. "Tiny's homecoming."

Grams patted the furry beast at her side and then walked happily from the room, Tiny following as close behind her as he could.

Sydney looked up at Brian, her eyes sparkling with laughter. "Are you trying to buy our affection, Mr. Hennesy?"

"Absolutely. Now come on," he grumbled as he wrapped his arm around her waist and ushered her out toward the back porch. "I need a partial return fast or I'm going to fall dead at your feet right here, and you'll have to get Tiny to lug me out of your lives."

Never. The word jumped into her head without thought or provocation, and she had to bite it back to keep from saying it aloud. And then she swallowed hard on the uncertainty that trailed immediately after such thoughts, and she followed Brian into the deepening night.

* * *

Brian had found a special restaurant twenty miles from town. It was naturally elegant, he said. Perfect for his two ladies.

Although Grams's appetite was tiny, her eyes were large with delight as they walked into the luscious surroundings and were seated on soft, peach-colored chairs at a wide table near a window. In the distance the black night stretched out endlessly, but just outside the wide expanse of windows, small lights positioned on the ground illuminated towering trees. A lovely stone-slabbed patio lay between.

Inside, the lighting was soft and dreamy and cast shadows on the muted wallpaper. Fine paintings added color to the room, and pieces of antique maple furniture—armoires and handsome secretary desks and small tables—held pots of flowers and hand-crafted statues. From the lounge on the other side of the restaurant, a classical guitarist was strumming romantic sounds of "Villa Lobos."

"This is grand," Sydney breathed. "They've kept the naturalness of the countryside but dropped this elegance right into the middle of it."

"I never knew such a place existed," Grams said, sipping from her crystal glass of sherry.

"It's new," Brian said. "I talked to the owner the other day."

"Why here?" Sydney asked.

"Why not?" Brian shrugged. "This is an ideal area. Look around the room. He said he was booked solid tonight."

"And your charm got us this perfect table?" Sydney felt slightly uncomfortable, but she couldn't put her finger on why.

Brian only laughed at her remark and ordered the fresh-oyster appetizer for all of them. "In the winter this place will be filled with skiers. And other times of year with people like us, who love the area for different reasons. The guy was smart. It's a wonderful investment."

Investment. That's what brought the disconcerting tugs. Reminders. And because of her feelings toward Brian, she couldn't even think straight about it all anymore, couldn't figure how she thought about anything. She sipped her wine slowly and sat quietly while the pale amber liquid soothed her, and Grams and Brian entertained each other in the distance.

By dinner's end she had buried her twinges beneath the feel of Brian's hand gently massaging her knee under the table and the marvelous chocolate mousse that even Grams had indulged in for dessert.

Later, Brian insisted on keeping his promise. After driving them home, he hung his sport coat over a chair, rolled up his shirt sleeves and tugged down seventeen boxes from Grams's stuffy, musty attic.

"There," he said, slapping his hands together and sending dust motes flying through the air. "That should keep you busy for ten years, Hortense." He looked at her sternly. "But if you dare put them back by yourself, you're in deep trouble. Tiny may walk out on you. And at the least, he'll let me know."

The dog flopped his tail heavily. He had not left Grams's side since they'd returned home from dinner. He seemed to crave her nearness and affection, and at the same time he stood guard.

Sydney watched it all in awe. She didn't even like dogs particularly. But Tiny was a loving member of the family already, and every time she looked at Grams's sparkling eyes and thought of Brian's part in it all, she felt nicely full.

"What do you want me to do with this sewing machine, Hortense?" Brian was asking in the distance. "It's a lost cause, I'm afraid. I pulled it out of the attic with the other stuff."

Grams looked at the ancient dusty Singer, and nostalgia swept across her face.

"Did you sew, Grams?" Sydney asked, walking over to the lopsided machine. Brian came up behind her and slipped two fingers into the waistband of her challis skirt. He rubbed slowly back and forth.

Grams shook her head, laughing, oblivious to the spears of fire traveling up her granddaughter's spine. "No, I certainly didn't. But my mother thought all young ladies needed a sewing machine in the corner of the parlor in order to get a husband."

Brian laughed. "Well, do you want to keep it?"

"I don't suppose I do. And I don't imagine Sydney has much use for it. She doesn't believe old wives' tales like that any more than I do. Right, darling?"

Sydney worked to concentrate over the sensuous play of Brian's fingers on her lower back. "Old wives' tales? Oh, no." She laughed, slightly embarrassed. And then she tightened the muscles of her face and grew practical to cool the hot waves of air floating around her. "Why don't we store it in the barn, Grams, until someone can come get it? Better than hoisting it back up into that attic."

"Good idea," Brian said, and Grams nodded agreement sleepily.

"Just don't disturb Asparagus and the new kittens, dear ones. Tiny and I are going to retire now, I think."

Brian watched the old woman and the dog walk from the room together. She was quite a lady, he thought. And no one had called him *dear one* for many, many years. It all fit into this whole big picture that was being painted around him. But he still wasn't quite sure where *he* would be able to fit into it. Shaking away the disturbing thoughts, he focused on Sydney.

She was standing quietly, dusting off the old sewing machine.

"Want to move it out tonight?" he asked, tracing an invisible line below her ear. He found that standing near Sydney meant touching her, no matter how lightly. It was as automatic as breathing. That kind of gentle, natural contact was new to Brian, whose life had always been so caught up in telephones and contracts, and he found it refreshingly intimate.

"If you don't mind," Sydney said. "That way she won't be tempted to do it herself."

Brian lifted the heavy machinery with little effort, and Sydney moved quickly ahead of him to hold open doors. Outside, the brick pathway to the barn was lighted by the moon and the two made their way easily to the broad wooden doors. Sydney lifted the heavy latch and opened the creaking doors.

"Is there a light?" Brian whispered.

"Just this one," she whispered back, flicking a switch on the wall. Soft yellow light coming from a single bulb filled the entryway to the barn. The rest of the echoing space was dark with black shadows cavorting along the rough walls.

"Good enough," he said softly, and slowly carried the cumbersome sewing machine over to a space against the wall.

Sydney stood inside the door and watched the marvelous play of muscles across his back as he worked. They bunched and loosened, then smoothed out as he set the machine down and stood up straight. He'd left his tie at the house and unbuttoned his shirt enough to reveal the dark thatch of hair beneath. The crease in his pants had disappeared during his numerous trips to the attic, and to Sydney he looked wonderfully and sensuously disheveled. The thought brought a grin to her face, but her eyes remained glued to his body. Lord, she was becoming a nymphomaniac.

Brian wiped his hands off on a rag hanging from a nail on the wall. "Well, that's that," he said softly.

"Why do you suppose we're whispering?" she asked quietly.

"Because—" Brian moved to her side "—there are monsters cavorting in the hayloft, making wild, passionate love, and we don't want to disturb them." His last words were whispered huskily into her ear.

"How do you know?"

"Because that's what haylofts are for. Not only monsters, but ghosts, teenagers, woodland creatures, cats, all sorts of wise beings make use of them." He laid his hands flat on the gentle slope of her shoulders while he talked.

"How do you know so much about haylofts?" Sydney asked, a kind of brazenness riding along the crest of her building emotion. In the darkness she could see light spilling from his black eyes. At this precise moment, she'd gladly step into any kind of fairyland he chose.

Brian's hands slipped up to her neck and on either side of her face his thumbs gently rotated on the smooth skin of her cheeks. "How do I know all about haylofts? Hmm, that's a tough one—you'll have to give me a minute."

Sydney laughed. "Now I, on the other hand, am intimately familiar with haylofts, and this one in particular."

"I see," Brian growled against her cheek. "Would the lady care to explain?"

She looped her arms around his waist as they stood still in the flickering yellow light. Sweet-smelling hay wafted around them and the shadowy magic of the moving light created an otherworldly feeling. "This lady knows the best loft to jump from and at what precise angle and how many bales need to be spread beneath to comfortably break the fall. I was quite a tomboy in my day."

Brian thought of the wondrous femininity beneath his fingers and had difficulty with the image. "A champion hayloft jumper, huh?" He kissed the top of her head. "Show me, my champion, of what you speak."

"The side loft is lower, easier to handle," she said, taking his hand from her face and leading him into the shadows to the left of the door. "You climb up there—" she pointed to a ladder against the wall and the hole at the top "—and then you jump into this soft nest right here at our feet."

"That's it?"

She nodded. Her face was flushed with the peculiar combination of emotions: the memories of childish delight and the incredible sensual vibrations passing between the two of them. Those emotions stirred and lighted new fires that made her wonder if there was a blue glow about her lighting up the whole barn.

"Show me." Brian stood still, his hands at his sides, his eyes intent on her.

"Now?"

He nodded.

"One of Grams's rules was never to jump with a dress on if there were boys around."

"Well—" his eyes slid over the silky blouse and skirt "—I suppose we could take care of that without too much difficulty."

Sydney headed quickly for the ladder. "I don't suppose that rule holds for mature adults."

"I shouldn't think." He watched her disappear into the shadows then appear again on the small loft.

"Any monsters up there?"

"If so, they're being *very* quiet."

"That's a shame. No passion. Are you ready to jump?"

"Yep. Here, take my shoes." She slipped out of the forest-green high-heeled shoes and tossed them down to Brian. "Ready?"

Brian smiled up into the shadows. Before him a thick blanket of new hay padded the floor. "I'm ready if you are."

"Then here I come." Grabbing the sides of her skirt, Sydney flew off the edge of the loft.

The collision was inevitable. He and Sydney were like two magnets that couldn't be kept apart. One step forward was all it took and she fell directly on him, and the two tumbled, tangled together, onto the silky bed of hay.

"Brian," Sydney breathed, brushing golden blades of straw from her face, "are you all right?" She was pressed tightly to his chest, her legs wrapped around him and her skirt tangled up around her waist.

His arms held her tightly. "All right?" He grinned at her. "I'm in heaven." The straw had shifted beneath his weight, and a soft, carved hollow held the two of them as perfectly as nature could have planned it.

"I...I don't look very ladylike," Sydney whispered. "Now I know why Grams had that rule."

"You look every bit the lady," Brian said softly. "My perfect lady." He stroked her hair gently, wondering if the feeling he had at this precise moment was complete happiness. If not, it came close. Her body was soft and pliant and restful against his chest. The tension of getting to know each other was gone, and left was this perfect kind of symmetry. It made him think of Sydney's photographs, and he smiled lovingly into her hair. She'd brought symmetry into his whole life.

"Do you think the monsters will be upset that we're invading their space?" Sydney asked. When she lifted her head from his chest to look at him, a stray moonbeam slipped through the window beneath the loft and lighted his smile.

"I don't think so. The kind that occupy these places are usually the magnanimous sort."

"Good." Sydney shifted her position on his body until her head was inches from his. "Then it's okay for me to kiss you."

"Absolutely." Brian's murmur was hushed as her lips pressed down and the tip of her tongue traced the familiar outline of his lips. He shuddered beneath the open intimacy of her kiss and the raw passion he felt pass back and forth between them. The heat of their desire swept them both up, supported them, held them together on the coolness of the hay.

"I've never felt this way before," Sydney murmured. "It's almost frightening—"

Brian nodded, pulling glinting pieces of straw from her hair. "It feels bigger than we are, doesn't it? That's the awesome part."

The awesome part for Sydney was that it was love, a deep, ebbing love that was taking over every inch of her—but she didn't say that. She rolled to one side of him, one leg still tangled between his, and looked up into the face that was a permanent part of her mind. She traced his lips with her fingertip, and he nipped lightly at her finger.

"We're like two smoldering bonfires; one little match and we flare up." His hand traveled the length of the long leg looped over his body and slipped up beneath her bunched skirt.

"That's kind of dangerous with all this hay around," Sydney said thickly.

"I was once a volunteer fireman. We're safe."

Sydney tried to respond with a skeptical look, but his hand had dipped beneath the elastic band of her panties, and his fingers were cupping over the melting center between her thighs. She struggled for a breath.

"I was sixteen," he said unevenly, "and was pretty good at putting out fires. But I think I've lost my touch."

"You haven't lost your touch." Quickly Sydney unfastened the buttons of his shirt. She wasn't sure who did what, but in seconds their clothes were in a pile and they lay together naked on the shining, golden blanket of straw.

Brian leaned over to her, his hips pressed tightly to hers. The moonlight spilled from her eyes. "You are so beautiful, Sydney. So wonderful—" He stroked her, lightly at first, his fingers circling her breasts and teasing the nipples to hardness. He traced the strips of moonlight across their swelling softness and down her belly to where they disappeared into the burnished tufts of hair.

Sydney stayed still beneath the amazing pleasure of his hands on her skin for as long as she could, and then her hands moved to his chest and matched him, touch for touch. His heartbeat beneath her fingers fueled her exploration, and she lovingly rubbed her palms across the coarse hairs on his chest and down to the smoothness of his abdomen, and then lower still until Brian moaned, his warm breath tickling her ear.

Sydney answered by sliding over him, her hands weaving into his hair, her body ripe and moist and welcoming when he came smoothly into her.

Bathed in moonlight, they moved slowly together in the rhythm of love. "Oh, my love," Brian breathed raggedly.

And then words stopped as they soared far beyond haylofts and barn and into a whole galaxy of wonderment until the moon burst around them. "My love," was the last thing Sydney heard before they both fell into a deep, moonlit slumber.

Ten

—

"Sleeping in the path of the moon is a cause of madness," Sydney said to no one in particular. She was alone, standing in the makeshift darkroom she had put together in the basement of her grandmother's house, but her mind refused to zero in on the task at hand. Instead it was all caught up on moonbeams and straw and dreams far too fevered to be caged up in a tiny room. Her darkroom had always been a getaway, a place where she could be alone and put things in order, but today it wasn't working that way. It made her feel claustrophobic.

"I am going crazy, I'm sure of it," she complained to the harsh chemicals as she carefully snapped a photo on the line to dry. "I should be upstairs on that phone, tracking down seventy-five thousand dollars, that's what I should be doing."

She looked carefully at one of the photos and her face broke into a brilliant smile. It was the series she'd taken that day out at the pond. She'd never gotten the harlequin ducks, but she had inadvertently snapped Brian at the exact second when he had tumbled right into Candlewick Pond, clothes and all. The camera had captured the look on his face, handsome even in its astonishment, and a thin shower of glistening water drops covering the whole photo gave it a surreal effect.

She looked at it more carefully, her mind wandering beyond the photographic aspects of the picture. It was amazing, she thought. In the time that had flowed from this one frozen moment, she had fallen in love.

Had it even been on that particular day? No, she had been attracted to Brian right from the start, but she didn't love him then. Her mind rolled over the days and moments and hours, but they all blended into a single feeling, and she couldn't isolate the precise moment. All she knew for certain was that she was tottering on the brink of a happiness so grand that it frightened her. And she didn't know how long she'd been there or how long she would stay, because time seemed irrelevant.

She looked once more at the picture, then tightly capped all her chemicals and washed her hands in the sink. Time to go about other business, she decided determinedly, and opened the door to leave. Tiny was sitting outside, a white bulging envelope attached to his keg.

"So you also work for Western Union, huh, Wonder Dog?" Sydney grinned and scratched the docile creature beneath his folds of chin. "Thanks."

When she opened the envelope, a spray of yellow straw fell to her feet. She looked again. It was *hay*, a whole golden shower of it. She looked into the few stray pieces remaining in the envelope and pulled out a square white card. "We made hay while the moon shone" was scrawled across it in bold black handwriting. Then "Love, Brian" appeared in the lower right-hand corner.

Sydney smiled into the happiness that spilled out of her. It was the closest he'd come to mentioning love. Exactly what that meant, however, she'd have to deal with later. She tucked the envelope into a pocket of her jeans and walked upstairs.

"Grams, where's Brian?"

"He had a meeting at the inn, darling." She sat at the kitchen table sorting through the final box from the attic.

"You didn't call me up."

Grams's white head moved back and forth. "No, he came to see me, Sydney."

"I see." Sydney slipped down beside Grams and cupped her chin in her hands. "And did the two of you have a good visit?"

"We did."

"And?"

Grams slipped off her glasses and looked at Sydney directly. "It was a little tête-à-tête, darling."

Sydney smiled and fingered an old comb that had fallen from one of the boxes. "So you talked about me," she said quietly.

"You confuse Brian in some ways, dear. But we had a lovely talk." Grams sat up straighter, dismissing the topic. Her brows drew into a small frown as she moved on to other things. "Sydney, it seems to me we need to move full steam on the inn, pull out all the stops. There isn't much time left."

Grams looked so frustrated Sydney almost forgot her own worry about the money that she still needed. She patted Grams's hand and tried to assure her it would work out.

"How much more?" Grams asked.

Sydney glanced at her wristwatch. "Actually, Grams, I'm not exactly sure. I'm meeting today with Gus's lawyer, Don Hendricks, and we're going to go over all the time-share contracts and the loans I've come up with, and then we'll know precisely." She felt suddenly guilty, as if somehow the time with Brian had been stolen from working toward the inn, in spite of the fact that she'd tracked down many dozens of leads and approached nearly every friend and family connection she had ever had. But Grams was right: there wasn't much time left.

"Are you very short, sweet pea?"

Sydney shrugged. "I think about seventy-five thousand. That's not insurmountable. We still have a few days."

Grams started to say something, then shook her head wearily. "If only I wasn't getting old, Sydney."

Sydney hugged her tightly. "Grams, your age has absolutely nothing to do with this. It will all work out."

"But it does," Grams insisted stubbornly. "My memory, you see, it fades when I need it most!"

Sydney had rarely seen Grams angry, but she was now, and Sydney couldn't for the life of her figure out why. The image was so incongruous, she had to bite back a smile. "Well, memory or not, I'll give it that Spencer try, right darling?"

The thought pleased Grams, and the worry lessened in her face. "Correct, and Tiny and I will be here to help."

Sydney hugged her again and ran up the stairs to slip into a skirt for her meeting. Not that anyone around Greenbriar cared, but she felt somehow it would bring her good luck. Maybe she'd even wear her challis skirt—

On a sudden impulse, she dashed down to the darkroom before leaving. She pulled the picture of Brian from the line and slipped it into a manila envelope, then dropped it into her valise. She'd stop by the inn on the way home and give it to him as a memento.

The news from Don Hendricks was what Sydney had expected. She was a little more than seventy-five thousand short, but the rest was all tight and secure.

"I have to admit, Sydney, I didn't think you could do it. This is a fine job here. If you ever need a job, I wouldn't mind someone with your drive around this office." He neatly bit the tip from a cigar and lighted up.

Sydney slipped her papers into her valise. "Thanks, Mr. Hendricks, but I haven't pulled this off yet. I still need a hefty sum of money." Her brows worked into a worry line. "And frankly, I don't have too many favors left to pull in."

Don smiled and patted her hand benevolently. "Well, Sydney, I hope you can pull it off. This town won't be the same without Candlewick. Now tell me, assuming as we all are that you'll do it, what in tarnation are you going to do with it? You're a photographer, not an innkeeper. And much as I love Hortense, she sure as hell—pardon my French, young lady—can't handle an inn."

Sydney laughed through the thin blue smoke and then grew serious as she considered the question. "To tell the truth, I don't know what I'm going to do. I guess I'll find someone to manage it. I'd love to use it as my home base, but I'd like to be free to leave when I have assignments. I haven't had a whole lot of time to think about it, actually."

"Nope, you sure haven't had a heck of a lot of time."

A light began to shine in Sydney's head. "Say, you don't suppose we could get a tiny extension on this, do you?"

Don Hendricks took a long draw off his fat cigar and shook his head firmly. "No, I don't. As a matter of fact I talked to Gus and Hennesy yesterday, and the meeting is set for twelve noon Friday. Goodlin and Hennesy's lawyers will be here just in case, and that's the way it's planned. Only person I can see who could extend it would be Brian Hennesy. And it seems you'd be the best one to convince him." He grinned as if he held the secrets to the universe, and Sydney blushed in spite of herself.

"No, no, I couldn't do that." There wasn't any way she could put her relationship with Brian in the middle of this. Things were confused enough as it was. Besides, they had agreed long ago to keep things separate.

"Well, then, that's that," the elderly lawyer said. "Twelve noon on Friday."

That's that. Twelve noon. The words hung heavy in the air as Sydney walked out of the Hendricks Brothers law offices and headed down Main Street. She was so preoccupied she almost forgot the photo for Brian, but the sight of the winding Candlewick driveway jarred her memory, and she walked quickly up the winding road, the thought of seeing Brian easing her more pressing concerns.

"Hey, Gus, how are you?"

"Fit as a fiddle, Sydney."

"And Ellie?"

"Mighty fine. Having this cabin has put life back into her, Sydney. She's even looking forward to the move to Arizona, long as she can come back from time to time. Now the icing on the cake would be if Candlewick were standing here when we returned."

Sydney felt the squeeze around her heart. "Well, I'm trying, Gus."

"I know you are, honey. And—" he slapped his fist down on the registration desk for emphasis "—don't think we aren't damned appreciative! Now, I suppose you're wanting to see Brian?"

"Just for a minute. Is he around?"

"Matter of fact, he just came down from his room. He and a city fellow are meeting in the library."

"Business?" Sydney's brow lifted and she looked toward the far doors opening into the paneled room.

"Don't rightly know, but they're only having coffee now so I think you should pop on in—"

Sydney smiled her thanks. "I just want to give him this—" she waved the envelope in the air "—and then I'll disappear."

The phone rang, and Gus reached for it as Sydney walked curiously toward the library door. It was the first time, as far as she knew, that Brian had had visitors out at Candlewick; he usually went into the city to handle things.

One of the French doors was open, and Sydney paused for a moment, wondering if a knock was appropriate. She could hear a voice coming from within, but it wasn't familiar. As she lifted her hand, she heard Brian's voice.

"I'm not sure, Jim. I don't know how much she has."

"Now that's not very savvy of you. I thought that's why you were hanging around here."

Sydney's heart froze.

"Jim, I explained all that—" Brian's voice was low and she could barely make out what he was saying, but the stranger's voice continued strong and loud as tiny pinpricks of fear traveled up Sydney's spine. She knew she should leave, but her feet were glued to the hardwood floor.

"Well, whatever…staving her off for thirty days like this was a damn stroke of genius. We'll get the money for the property tomorrow, but being able to wait until that note was due benefited us even more than we thought. Good job, Hennesy!"

The thunder in her ears nearly blocked out the sound of someone slapping someone else on the back, but Sydney had heard too much already. She thought for a moment she was going to be sick, but a long draw of air steadied her enough to walk across the lobby toward the front door.

Gus was coming out of his small office behind the desk. "Hey, missy, did you see our young man?"

Sydney looked at him blankly. The insidious weight inside her was growing large, blocking out all feeling and sense. "Pardon me?"

"*Brian*, Sydney. Did you see Brian?"

"No," she said calmly. "I didn't see him."

"You okay, Sydney?" Gus peered over his bifocals.

It was when she tried to smile that she felt the painful pressure of tears—huge, choking torrents of tears. She nodded briskly that she was fine and hurried out the door, too blind to see the envelope slip from her hands or to hear Gus calling to her to wait. She walked straight ahead, out, away, anywhere.

She ended up down at the creek, although she didn't know how she'd gotten there. She sat at the edge, her feet hanging limply over the bank, her eyes staring straight ahead but seeing nothing.

Bits and pieces of words pierced painfully through her consciousness. *Hanging around. Staving her off. Good job, Hennesy.* They grew louder and louder until Sydney covered her ears to block out the deafening sounds. And then all was still, and the only sound stretching out over the water and being washed downstream was the growing, painful sobbing of Sydney's grief.

"Sydney, dear, it's time to eat. Come, we need company." Grams sat at the kitchen table, dropping bits of ham into Tiny's gaping mouth.

"One more phone call, Grams." She dialed the phone fiercely, while her free hand scribbled notes on a yellow pad.

She'd allowed herself exactly one day to mourn, during which she'd sought refuge with her camera out in a quiet wooded area of Green Mountain where the photos would be beautiful and where Brian Hennesy would never find her.

Her heart fought back again and again against the knowledge that Brian had used her as a convenient pastime and a ticket to a better deal. Yet she knew what she had heard. But there had been some feeling in their relationship, and nothing could convince her to believe anything different. She knew people too well. Brian had cared for her, maybe even as much as he was capable of caring for anyone. But it wasn't the deep, committed love that she had felt in their lovemaking, that had become the substance of her dreams. And now it made sense that marriage had never been mentioned. Brian would never marry her, and probably would never marry anyone.

She was as angry with herself as with the rest of mankind. She knew enough of the world to know what men were like. Look at her own father. He'd used plenty of women—probably even her own mother, just as her mother had used him. She should have seen this for what it was from the very beginning.

Use. The word echoed painfully in her head and pushed more tears to the surface until Sydney was limp. She couldn't even blame Brian for not loving her. He'd never promised her a thing.

But what gave Sydney the energy she needed to move ahead was the knowledge that whatever feeling Brian might have had made no difference in the long run. Because at rock bottom was the fact that he *had* deceived her. He had never for one moment thought she would get the money she needed. So he'd watched her, played with her, loved her, while he'd waited out his time. And he'd never let on for a moment.

The shame and anger that washed over her dried her tears and strengthened her resolve. She *would* get the inn, even if she had to hold up a Wells Fargo truck to do it. And then she'd get on with her life.

"Sydney?"

"Yes, Grams." She shoved the yellow pad into her valise and walked slowly to the table.

"Brian called again."

Sydney had told Grams just enough to explain why Brian was out of her life, but had tried to spare her all the sordid details. "I don't understand why he persists."

"He cares."

Sydney was silent.

"He doesn't understand, Sydney. He looks awful. Why don't you at least talk to him?"

"Grams," Sydney said patiently, "I would if there was a reason to. But there isn't anything to say. Brian knows everything." She felt the tears rising to the surface again. It was when she talked to Grams that the pain was especially bad, because in a way Brian had deceived Grams as well. He'd come into her life and Grams had made a place for him there, and now she had to painfully tear him from it. And he shouldn't have done that; he had no right.

"Sweet pea, I'm so sorry," Grams said softly. She rose from the table and moved to Sydney's side. And then she wiped away her granddaughter's tears and held her to her soft bosom, just as she'd done when Sydney was a child.

* * *

Sydney stood in the darkroom and flicked the switch off so that she could develop the negatives of her latest roll of film. They weren't important pictures, just some of Tiny she thought might cheer up Grams, but she thought an hour away from her figures might bring back some balance so she could dive in renewed. No matter how she worked the numbers, she still came up fifty thousand dollars short. And there were only three days left.

Carefully she opened the roll of film and slipped it into the first solution.

She didn't hear the footsteps nor the doorknob turning, but when it was jerked open with such force that the light on the ceiling shook, Sydney froze.

"We're going to talk, damn it, whether you want to or not." Brian took one long step into the room and filled the only escape route. He didn't touch her, just stood there powerfully, his eyes darkening to the steely blue of a stormy sea.

The sight of him after an absence of nearly four days nearly overwhelmed her. He looked tired, with deep shadows beneath his eyes and a drop to his jaw that was unlike him. Sydney braced herself against the counter. "You...you shouldn't have come barging in like that. You've ruined my film." She didn't want the tears to come, not in front of him. If she could only hold off for a brief moment—

"And *you're* trying to ruin a hell of a lot more!" The force of his voice was too much for the tiny space, and it ballooned out into the hallway. Brian stood still, his feet planted apart, and looked down at the floor, concentrating. Then he looked up at Sydney, and when he spoke again, his voice was strained but under control. "I'm sorry. I don't usually get like that. Sydney, I need very much to talk to you."

When she started to shake her head and move around him, he grasped her shoulders and held her still. "You owe me at least that."

"I don't owe you anything." The sudden spurt of anger was a blessing. It seemed to glue her tightly together.

"Yes, you do," he said. "We've shared a great deal. And that brings some responsibilities with it."

"I don't think you're one to talk about responsibilities." She was surprised when her voice reached her ears. It was cool and direct, the voice of a woman in control. That was such an irony, when her insides felt like a pile of ashes that would soon blow away.

"I know what happened, Sydney. Gus gave me the picture and told me you'd been there. So I assume you heard Jim Goodlin and me talking. I can only guess what part or how much you heard, but I'm going to fill you in."

"No need." Sydney looked down intently at the tips of her tennis shoes.

"Oh yes, there *is* need. I love you, Sydney, dammit!"

Sydney's heart lurched at the words, but she held herself firm. It was a little late for protestations. "You have a funny way of showing love, Brian. The fact is, you deceived me. You stayed here and watched over me and played with me because in the end you'd wind up richer. It was a wonderful business deal." She lifted her head and felt the moisture collecting in the corners of her eyes, but she held her head still, her chin tilted firmly upward. "That's a perverted kind of love, Brian."

Brian winced. He took a deep breath and then spoke in measured tones. "I did originally give in to your request for the extension for those reasons. And I suppose I stayed around partly because of that. But the part that you failed to mention was the surprise that happened during those days. The fact that I fell in love. I never intended that to happen. But it did, honestly and openly, and no matter what you say, I know you love me, too."

Sydney was silent. She didn't think it possible that fingernails and eyebrows could hurt, but they did. Every millimeter of her body hurt. "Whatever I feel...felt...it doesn't matter, because the plain truth is you tricked me and all be-

cause it made good business sense to do so. If not in the beginning, you could have told me later on, Brian—set the
record straight—'' Her voice started to break, and she
stopped short.

"Why, Sydney? Why should I have told you at any point?
It was business, just as the plan you had for getting the
money for Candlewick Inn was business, and we didn't discuss that. Don't you see? I could have said something, sure.
And maybe I should have, although it wasn't exactly the
kind of thing to bring up in casual conversation. But it had
absolutely nothing to do with you and me. It didn't affect
what you did—''

"It damn well did!" Sydney cried, the tears falling read-
ily now. "Not knowing let me fall in love with you. I would
never, ever have done that if I had known what this was all
about!''

Brian's hands dropped from her shoulders, and a look of
forced calm settled over his face. Mixed in was a sadness
that tore at Sydney's heart. "Sydney, I've been thinking a
great deal about a lot of things these days. I know how you
love Candlewick Inn. Believe it or not, I love it, too. But I
think this business deal isn't the whole story. I think you're
hiding behind it. I think falling in love with me frightened
you. I've seen it in your eyes and the way your body moves
at different times. I've even talked to Grams about it.

"I don't quite understand why, but I think you're using
the inn to protect yourself from something. Every time I get
too close, you pull it out and shove it right there between us.
Maybe you need to put a little thought into that, and face up
to something yourself, darlin'. I think it might make a difference.''

Sydney stared up at him, pulling anger tightly around her.
"Oh, you think that, do you? You don't think I could honestly have problems with the fact that you are willing to
participate in this whole deal, especially now that you know
this town and the people in it? You don't think that maybe

I don't like people like you? Well, you're wrong, Brian Hennesy!''

"I've been wrong in my life, and I've admitted it, but this time I don't think I am. The sad part is, I can't do anything about it. The ball's in your court, Sydney."

"Well, here's something in your court that may cheer you up some. I may not get the money I need for the inn, after all. I'm still over fifty thousand dollars short, as you probably know. So you just might have the pleasure of signing those papers Friday and bringing in the wrecking crews.'' She closed her eyes and leaned against the counter. She couldn't talk anymore. She was totally exhausted, and logic had failed her a long way back. It was all too much, too tiring, too heartbreaking— Brian was still looking at her when she opened her eyes. It was a look of such fierce tenderness that Sydney almost cried out. But before she could say a word, Brian turned and walked away.

She stayed there for a moment, stunned, and then turned out the lights and groped her way upstairs. Grams had already gone to bed, and the house was eerily quiet. Numbly Sydney grabbed a down cover and stumbled onto the back porch. The wind was brisk but not too cold, and she curled her weary body into the soft cushions of the divan, wrapped the down comforter over her and, like a child who's too young to know any better, fell into a sound, dreamless sleep.

Eleven

It was the chill wind and the silence of dawn that woke Sydney hours later. The comforter had slipped off and lay beside the divan in a peach cloud, and outside, beyond the screened window, the earth was changing colors.

Her hand moved slowly to her forehead. Her head hurt, but the feeling of packed sawdust was gone. The tiredness, the helplessness, the inability to listen and sort and make sense of things was gone. Sleep had mercifully cleaned her out.

And then the past twenty-four hours slowly replayed themselves in her mind, hour by hour, word by word. And as she sorted through the turmoil of the day, the one emotion that inched its way back into her until it filled her almost to the point of pain, was her love for Brian Hennesy. It was there in rich, vivid Technicolor, filling every channel of her body.

She pulled the comforter from the floor and wrapped it around her shaking body, tugging it all the way up to her chin. And she stared out through the screens at the wonder of morning and the newness it created as the sky lightened. It was what Brian had done for her: created a newness in her, filled her and brought life to her. She pulled her knees up to her chin and felt the tears trickle down onto her cold hands.

The things she'd said to Brian yesterday haunted her. They'd been emotional outbursts, unbalanced. And they had driven away the man she loved.

At the creaking of the back door, she looked up and half smiled through puffy eyes at the sight of Grams, wrapped in a warm furry robe, shuffling out onto the porch. Tiny lumbered close behind her. "Here," Grams said, holding out a cup of coffee. "It's instant, but it will ward off the chill."

"Thanks, Grams," Sydney said softly. "I hope I didn't wake you."

"Nope. Couldn't sleep."

"You're worried about all this—the inn and Brian and all."

Grams's smile was tired. "I'm worried about you, sweetie. Do you love him?"

"Very much."

"Then tell him."

"I'm frightened, Grams." She turned her head until her cheek rested on her knee. "Frightened and not sure of myself at all. It's a peculiar sensation."

"It's because of your mother and father, isn't it?"

Sydney laid her head against the porch swing and closed her eyes. "That's always been hard for me to talk about."

"I know, Sydney, dear. I was around, remember?"

Sydney nodded. "Yes, you were always here, my safe haven."

"And you always insisted their unconventional life-style was great; you were the envy of every youngster at your school."

"I think I convinced the kids, too," Sydney said.

"But my sweet child, every youngster—even wild and woolly ones—need certain things in place in their lives. And Alana and Dick never seemed to be able to do that for you. Things were so whirlwind, romantic, harum-scarum—I've thanked the good Lord for twenty-seven years for watching out for you, because someone had to."

"But they loved me."

"Yes, they did. But you wanted a mother and father who also loved each other enough to make a commitment. And that you never had."

"I think Brian loves me," she began slowly.

"Brian loves you so much he carries it on his shirt sleeve. The whole town knows Brian loves you, my pet."

"But he's never mentioned marriage," she said in hushed tones. "And because he's who he is, it all seems so unlikely. And Grams—" her voice choked as feelings and cloudy emotions cleared in her mind "—I *won't* just be someone's longtime lover. I won't repeat what my parents did and chance bringing a child into that kind of relationship." She had never said it aloud before, never expressed the always-lurking fear she had of repeating her parents' patterns, of becoming her mother. She felt a surge of relief, a tremendous relief, sweep through her.

Grams watched her through misty eyes. "Did Brian suggest that sort of arrangement, Sydney?"

She shook her head miserably. "But with all those differences between us, I think it might have been the next step."

"Maybe that's not entirely fair to him," Grams suggested quietly. "I think some of these insights and fears need to be shared with him, don't you, love?"

Sydney felt the buildup of tears again, but she held them back this time. "I don't quite know what to do. I wasn't very nice to him, Grams."

"Some of your anger was justified. He knows that. And the rest can be worked out if you want it to be."

If she wanted it to be. There was nothing she wanted more in her life. There wasn't anything else that mattered. The myriad of problems—geographic and business differences and the like—faded into insignificance in the light of the love she felt for Brian Hennesy. She didn't know quite how all those problems would fall into place, but she knew as certainly as the sun was lifting over the treetops that she wouldn't be whole without Brian in her life.

"Go," Grams said quietly.

A quick shower took away the last remnant of sleep, and Sydney was at the inn door as the first flapjacks hit the huge cast-iron stove in the Candlewick kitchen.

"Gus," she said breathlessly as she walked into the lobby, "would you please ring Brian?"

"Lord, and aren't you up at the crack of dawn?" Gus took off his glasses and smiled warmly. "I could ring him, Sydney, but it wouldn't do much good."

Sydney's heart sank. "He's already up?"

"He left, Sydney. Yesterday. Threw a bunch of stuff in his car and took off. Said he'd be back with Goodlin for the meeting on Friday."

Sydney didn't trust her voice. She stood mutely, staring at the polished desktop.

"He was distressed about something when he left. But he did say I shouldn't worry. He'd take care of things. So you shouldn't worry, either, I don't suppose."

Sydney listened with half an ear. Brian was gone. She'd sent him away. He had stayed around because of her, and she'd taken that reason away from him.

Numb and sick at heart, she went back to the house and slumped down at the kitchen table. She was as drained and miserable as she had ever been in her life. As she stared unseeing at the stack of papers she had pulled from her valise, a small, pitiful laugh escaped. She had started out the month seeking balance to her life, and look at her now. A first-class failure in the balance department. And the outlook wasn't great.

Sydney squeezed her eyes shut and forced herself to breathe. She couldn't do anything about this now. She would have to suspend it all for the next few days. She owed this last thrust to Gus and Ellie and Grams and anyone else whose hopes had been raised by her magnanimous gesture. Maybe that's all she was: a shell of magnanimous gestures.

"Sydney, dear—"

Grams's thin voice invaded her self-pity, and she turned reluctantly to face her.

An old apron covered Grams from waist to knees, and she was wiping her hands on it. "Gus called me, and I know you're sitting here scolding yourself for numerous silly things. Love will hold out, but Candlewick Inn will not. Perhaps the best antidote is to forge ahead and find the money we need. And we'll worry about tomorrow, tomorrow."

Sydney felt a lifting inside her. She *was* feeling sorry for herself, which was really what Grams was saying in her kindly way. Besides, she couldn't deal with the pain of Brian right now. And she couldn't do anything about it, either. She brushed the back of her hand over a tangle of hair and smiled. "That old Spencer try—let's go for it."

For eight hours straight, Sydney held the phone to her ear and dialed an infinite combination of numbers. Grams attacked the New York phone directory and personal address books with the energy of a Boy Scout. The duo stopped only for tea and chocolate cake and a late dinner of carryout chicken.

"Grams, you're a trooper," Sydney said with a sigh as they finally stumbled up the stairs late that night.

"Not enough of one, Sydney." Her voice was firm and clear, without the tiredness that had laced it all day. "I'm a damn fool, that's what!" Tiny turned soulful eyes to his master.

"Grams, stop that! This whole thing is my bed, not yours. You've been a terrific help to me, darling, and I wouldn't have been able to get this far without you."

"This far is fifty thousand dollars short."

"But we have until noon tomorrow. And Grant Starke from my bank is talking to a group for me tonight. One person could do it, Grams." She forced every ounce of energy she had left into sounding optimistic.

Grams nodded without enthusiasm, kissed Sydney on the cheek and moved off to her room, mumbling about banks and treasurers.

Sydney fell into her bed, and only then, when the world was quiet and her eyes looked up into the blackness of the night, did she allow herself to think of Brian. She would still hold him tight, keep him close, until she was certain it was futile. She would sleep with him wrapped intimately in her thoughts, just as he was in her heart.

Grant Starke's call came at ten-thirty the next morning. "Sounds great, but not right now, and we wish you lots of luck" was the news.

Sydney swallowed a mouthful of hot coffee and barely felt the sting. Less that two hours left—and she had come so close. She'd almost done it.

At that moment Grams walked into the kitchen, a shawl wrapped tightly around her shoulders and her brows knit together. "Come, Sydney."

Sydney's head shot up in alarm. "Grams, what is it?"

"It's the barn. I'm sure of it now. Hurry up."

Before Sydney could question her further, Grams and Tiny were out the back door with Sydney following hastily.

"Sydney, hurry up," Grams shouted over her shoulder, and Sydney raced to her side, then grabbed her arm to slow her down.

"Grams, stop. You're going to have a heart attack!" Her heart beat wildly at Grams's erratic behavior.

"Sydney," Grams said huffily, "I didn't want to tell you this because you might think I was 'teched,' but I've done a foolish thing, child."

They'd reached the barn, and Sydney held the heavy door so that Grams and Tiny could enter. "Grams, please, what are you talking about?"

"It happened when Henry died, sweet pea, and your mother had just had you and was traipsing all over the world, and I needed some security, don't you see?"

"Yes, darling, I see." She didn't see at all, but maybe if she could get Grams to slow down, the older woman would feel better and make more sense. "Let's sit over here on a bale of hay, Grams."

Grams looked at Sydney sharply. "Sydney, we have very little time left; I don't think it wise to stop to chat!" Tiny drifted off, sniffing frantically at hay bales and boxes and old machinery packed into the barn. "See, Tiny knows."

"Grams," Sydney said softly, "I don't know what you're talking about. Can you explain?"

"It was the money, you see. Henry had a trust for me and your mother, but it was all in the bank and it didn't seem nearly as safe as having something close at hand. So when the life-insurance money came, I cashed it and stored it—"

"You . . . stored it?"

"Yes, sweet pea. I stored it all away somewhere. In case the trust fizzled or something happened, then I'd always have that lump of money ready to go. And I wanted it for you in case your mother didn't handle things the way a Spencer should, don't you see."

Sydney was beginning to, and with the realization came a rush of adrenaline. "Grams, are you saying you've hidden money in this barn?"

"It was so long ago, sweetie—" Grams's face clouded, and she looked over Sydney's shoulder. "I can't seem to pull it up out of the past. But I remember the smell, the smell of that clean, silky hay. Yet I've checked a dozen times and couldn't find a trace, so I checked the attic. All those boxes . . . and the closets—''

"Oh, Grams." Sydney didn't know whether to laugh or cry. She thought of Brian patiently dragging every box in the attic down for Grams's inspection. And neither of them ever suspected she was looking for a buried treasure. "How much money did you put away?'' It couldn't have been much, Sydney thought, or she would surely have banked it—

"I don't exactly remember, dear."

"But not much, was it?"

Grams's back stretched straight and tight. "Henry was a good provider. Not like some of the Hanovers. It was enough. But the issue is not how much is there but *where* it is, don't you see?''

"I think I do see, Grams." She felt a spray of hay fall on her head and looked up. Tiny had made his way up a ramp at one end of the back loft and was nuzzling his fat nose into piles of hay, scattering them.

"If you see, then why are you standing there instead of looking, Sydney? There is enough money there to buy Candlewick Inn. Now we must find it.''

Sydney's heart lurched. For one brief moment she thought of Brian and the pure delight he would find in the whole scenario, and then she grinned and rushed to the side of the barn to begin moving machinery and cartons and old sacks of wonderful-smelling pine chips.

"How much time?'' Grams called from behind a pile of harnesses that hadn't been moved in twenty years.

Sydney wiped a cobweb from her face and glanced down at her wrist. "Oh, Grams—only thirty-five minutes!''

For the next fifteen minutes, the only sound in the cavernous hollow was that of the wind whistling through worn boards in the side of the building and the clunk and crunch of objects being moved and hay being stepped on.

Sydney spotted Grams moving a heavy coil of wire and rushed to her side to help.

"There's no fool like an old fool, is there, Sydney?" Grams looked up at her sadly.

"How dare you say that! We have twenty minutes left, and we're not going to give up!" She planted a kiss on Grams's cheek and reached up at the same time to wipe away the hay that Tiny was shaking over the side of the loft. Her finger touched a wide, flat piece of paper. "Tiny, what the—" she scolded as she lifted her head, and then words died in her throat. Floating over the side of the loft in a gentle rain were hundreds of green bills, and standing proudly at the top was Tiny, a yellowed sack in his teeth and his head moving happily back and forth.

Twelve

The bills were large, mostly in denominations of five hundred and one thousand. Sydney shuddered. She'd never seen that much money in currency before. It was mind-boggling.

While Grams scooped the money into an empty box, Sydney rushed up the ladder and found another small sack that Tiny had unearthed from a hollow built into the side of an old tool cabinet. With the dog in tow, she collected both bags and tore down the steps. They made only one detour—a race into the house for Sydney's valise and one of Grams's empty knitting bags.

"We wouldn't want them to think we were haphazard," Grams said. She sounded younger, Sydney thought, than she had in a dozen years.

While Sydney drove the short distance to the inn, Grams counted out money until the knitting bag held fifty thousand dollars in currency. At the last minute, Grams stuck in five thousand dollars more. "Just for good measure," she said. The rest of the bills she stacked neatly, piled into the sack and shoved under the front seat. "For your dowry," she said with a twinkle in her eye.

It wasn't until they passed the Widow's Tavern that Sydney began to focus on reality again. In minutes she would see Brian. Her heart began to beat erratically, and she pressed the palm of her hand against her chest. Beyond seeing him, she didn't know what she would do, but he'd be there, they'd talk, and maybe somehow—

"Oh, gracious Lord!" Grams's voice filled the car and Sydney instinctively slammed on the brakes.

They both expelled a long breath and stared through the windshield.

Three fat, fawn-colored Guernsey cows were waddling slowly across the street. On the sidewalk and steps of the neighboring stores, small patches of people had collected, laughter lighting their faces and fingers pointing excitedly at the spectacle.

"Oh no," Sydney groaned. "Not now. Move cows!" She pressed down on the horn, but the cows seemed not to notice. Finally, after what seemed an interminable amount of time, she pulled the car close to the curb and slowly edged her way around the heavy bodies.

"Oh, Grams," she murmured, "What time is it?"

Grams's jaw was set and she looked straight ahead. "Just drive, Sydney, dear."

Sydney looked down at her own watch. Twelve-ten. Ten minutes late. Her heart pounded as she turned the wheels into the inn driveway, spinning gravel onto the freshly mowed lawns. She brought the car to a sudden halt right in the middle of the driveway, and in seconds she and Grams were up the stairs and walking across the lobby.

"In the library," Sydney said breathlessly.

No one noticed them at first when they walked through the library's wide double doors. The two women stopped, stunned for a moment, and scanned the room.

On the opposite wall was a huge stone fireplace, flanked on either side by a leather couch. On one, Gus Ahern and his wife Ellie sat bathed in broad smiles that lighted up the entire room. Opposite them, Brian Hennesy and Don Hendricks chatted amicably, each man puffing on a fat cigar. Between them, on the hand-carved coffee table, were legal-looking documents and several other slips of paper. There was no one else in the room.

Sydney's heart caught in her throat and then seemed to stop altogether. It didn't make any sense. Her eyes drifted to Brian. He had a suit on, just as he had that very first day. And again he seemed oblivious to it, his long, lanky body comfortably handsome in anything. Or nothing... His smile was beguiling, wonderful. Her heart began to pound again, and a warm rush of love surged freely through her.

"Sydney, dear, we ought to go in." Grams lightly touched her arm.

Sydney looked surprised at first, then nodded, relieved that someone else was able to make decisions. The other lawyer didn't seem to be there, nor the man Brian worked for. She couldn't put this all together right now, not with Brian sitting there, so close. All she wanted to do was wrap her arms around him and love him.

"Ladies!" Gus nearly leaped from the couch. "Congratulations!"

Sydney looked at him strangely. Then Don Hendricks stood and walked over to them. "What a wonderful coup, Sydney." He slapped one hand over his vest pocket and made a half bow. "Mr. Hennesy and I are celebrating with cigars, if anyone should care to join us." He laughed heartily, then ushered Grams to a seat near the coffee table.

"I can think of a much better way to celebrate."

The words were a deep whisper in her ear, and Sydney felt all the glue holding her together melt and ebb right out of her body. Brian's hand on the small of her back finished the job, and her knees slowly began to bend. "Gotcha," he said, and slipped one arm around her waist. He walked with her over to the couch and she slid down, welcoming the firm cushion beneath her.

"Brian, I don't know what's going on here," she said with as much strength as she could manage.

"Only good things," Brian assured her, his arm moving around to the back of the couch. He needed to touch her, to keep her there within reach. He'd never in his life wanted anyone this way, and he would fight heaven and hell to keep her a part of his life.

"Mr. Hendricks said the inn is yours, dear," Grams said, her wrinkled face beaming like the noonday sun. "And it happened before we ever arrived, it seems."

Sydney looked from one face to the other. "I don't understand this. Gus, I *do* have the money—but we were late because—"

Gus's head moved back and forth, his eyes glowing. "It's all right, Sydney. Don had all your documentation except for the fifty thou or so, and Brian here kicked that in; so Candlewick is now legally, officially yours, my dear."

It wasn't until she sat for a full minute with all eyes in the room focused directly on her that Gus's words registered. *Brian kicked in . . .*

She looked at him sideways. He was calm and relaxed, puffing on the cigar and watching her watch him.

"I didn't know you smoked cigars," she said finally.

"Only on special occasions."

"Brian, would you please tell me what's going on?"

"Gus just did. The inn is yours." His hand dropped down to her shoulders. "I guess I've been secretly rooting for you for a while now. And when it seemed you might not pull the necessary funds together, something clicked inside me. You were right, I *do* know these folks; they're my friends." He leveled a long look at her and added softly, "Friends—and far more. The whole damn place suddenly began to mean more to me than most other things. I guess I've done ten years or so of thinking in the past few days, and I've made some rather momentous decisions along the way. But we'll talk about that later. For now, the important thing is that the inn will stay put, maybe forever, with tender, loving care."

A resounding cheer went up in the room, and Brian laughed. "Well, I guess that's unanimous. I'm glad I'm on this side of the fence now."

"You are?" Sydney's voice was so low she wasn't sure he heard her.

"It's the only way," he said slowly, the color in his eyes turning a dangerous and familiar midnight blue.

Sydney's body reacted before she could catch a cooling breath. She curled her fingers around Grams's knitting bag.

"It seems our Brian just told Jim Goodlin what he could do with his contract," Grams said happily.

Brian's head fell back and he laughed deeply. "Well, Hortense, something like that, I guess."

"Brian," Sydney said, forcing her mind to concentrate on details, "even I know that wouldn't have been very wise. Wasn't he terribly angry?"

Brian half smiled, then shrugged. "Jim doesn't like to lose. But we had a long, tedious meeting. I bargained and he bargained. In the end he relaxed a bit and promised not to have me roughed up, and I agreed to handle one other job for him—an important deal he's been interested in out in Oregon."

"And that was that? That's all he said?"

"No. He also said I was crazy, but that you must be one hell of a woman. I said yes, you were."

Sydney bit down hard on her bottom lip. Her thoughts were flying in too many directions, and her heart wasn't cooperating at all. "Brian, what does it mean exactly, canceling out on the contract?"

"It kind of means I quit. Goodlin was my biggest client. It's pure irony, Sydney. I never cared a damn about spending money; it just kept piling up. And then the one time I wanted like hell to use it for something, my hands were tied." His brows had pulled together, but when he looked around the room, then back to Sydney, his face relaxed and his mouth crooked in a smile. "So I untied them."

"You sure as hell did!" Gus laughed merrily.

"Well, I'd say this deserves a celebration," Don Hendricks said as he lined up the papers and put them neatly into his attacheé. "We can get the necessary John Henrys on these later when Doris, my notary public, joins us. For now I'm treating all interested parties to champagne and ham steaks down at the Widow's place."

"A lovely idea!" Grams said, and a flurry of activity followed as people rose from their chairs and headed for the door, chatting happily.

"Mind if we're a little late?" Brian said, taking Sydney by the arm.

"We don't mind at all," Grams said, her small chin lifted high. "I should think you two need to get a few business details straightened out." She winked at Brian, then turned smartly and took Don Hendricks's outstretched arm.

Sydney looked up at Brian, suddenly afraid. This was it, then. Zero hour.

"Do you trust me enough to come up to my room for a minute? I forgot something up there I meant to give you."

Sydney started to speak, but the words got lost somewhere in her throat. She nodded.

They walked up the single flight of stairs in silence, Brian one step behind, guiding her with the sure touch of his fingers until the door was unlocked and she was ushered gently inside.

She looked around slowly. "I...I've never seen where you were staying. Strange, isn't it?" Strange and terribly sad. It was over. The thirty days...and he had already agreed to another job. A universe of unspoken words lingered between them.

"Do you want it?" Brian said finally, his eyes deep and burning. He didn't know what she'd say. The love was there, of that he was damn sure. But he wasn't sure if she could trust enough.

"Do I want what?" The tears must have been waiting all this time, she thought, blinking hard, because all of a sudden they were there, pressing tight against her lids.

"This—" Brian drew her over to the window seat and picked up a manila envelope. *Her* envelope—the one she'd dropped in the lobby a lifetime ago.

With shaking hands she opened the flap and pulled out the familiar picture. "Brian, I—" She started to tell him she understood, that she had accused him unjustly of being unfeeling, that he had done a wonderful thing, that she knew he had to move on, that she loved him but— But then she noticed the black writing, like a hurried autograph, scrawled across the image of Brian flying into the pond.

"Would you marry this man?" she read.

The tears that were ready erupted on cue.

"Here, darlin'." He took her by the shoulders and turned her toward him. "I love you, Sydney, more than I can begin to say. So I want to borrow a lifetime, and that might be enough for a start—" He crooked his finger beneath her chin and lifted her face to his. "What do you say?"

A small smile quivered across her lips. "You want to know if I'd marry a guy who scares off rare ducks and falls in ponds?"

"And absolutely craves your body..." He kissed away a teardrop meandering down her cheek and wove his fingers into her hair. "And that's not all," he growled. "But I want to save some surprises for later. I love you, Sydney. I love you, I love you, I love you—" His hands held her head still while he nuzzled her neck fiercely between each "I love you."

"Brian, I'm having trouble grasping all this. Maybe we need to go back to the beginning." Her eyes sought an assurance in his that she couldn't put into words.

Brian's hands slipped around her back, and he fitted her body to his. "Of time? I think I'm there, darlin'. It's all just beginning for us...if you want it to be." He pulled away slightly then, looking down into her eyes. Here he'd made a small fortune putting fancy deals together by reading people's minds and motives, and he was as anxious as a kid on Christmas Eve, wondering if Santa would really come through this year.

"We'll start slowly," Brian said patiently, his hand feeling its way up and down her spine. "Do you love me?"

She burrowed her head into his shoulder. "I thought you were the mind reader. Of course I love you."

"Good, I thought so." He brushed a kiss above her ear. "Item number two: I know you were mad as hell at me, Sydney, about the inn deal and the thirty days' wait. It *was* business, and if you had been anyone but you, my silence would have been perfectly legitimate, but you were right. I realized that when I was driving like a maniac back to New York. I should have said something when the feelings between us took over the way they did. I owed you that. I owed you that because I loved you."

When Sydney looked up she saw genuine sadness in his eyes.

"I'm not used to that," he continued. "To balancing personal responsibilities and business."

"It's okay," she said softly.

"I hope so." His fingers stroked her hair. "But there's a third item here. Numero three." He lifted her hand to his lips and kissed the soft pads of three fingers. "It's this thing you have about commitment. I finally figured it out."

"Brian, I—"

"Wait, let me give it a try. It's important to me, Sydney, to understand the things that are important to you."

She nodded against his shoulder and wondered how she could have lived twenty-seven years without this love that now seemed so essential to the simplest of tasks.

"I know your childhood wasn't the Disney World you talk about it being—or maybe it was—but it was the kind of place that's nice to visit but not so nice to live in."

She smiled slowly. "That's fair."

"And I want you to know before we go any farther—" he lifted her chin up until she looked directly into his eyes "—that I understand that. I don't want a wild and crazy relationship. I want *you*—I want to marry you—*forever*... and to fill my arms and my heart with little bodies that look exactly like you."

"When does the woman get to talk?"

"Soon, love, soon." His kisses fell like raindrops along her hair. "After the woman says yes."

"Oh, Brian, you know I'll marry you. If you hadn't asked, if you'd hadn't come back—"

"—then there wouldn't be any sense in this world at all. I'd be a damn fool. You're the best thing that has ever happened to me."

"Even though I seem to have already cost you a small fortune? First the money you put into the inn, then your commission—"

"Hmm," he said, pulling her closer, "you do owe me a thing or two, don't you? Okay, how about a job?"

Sydney pulled from his arms and shifted on the seat so that she could see his face. "What are you talking about?"

"Hire me as Candlewick's new innkeeper. Gus said he'd write me a glowing letter of recommendation."

"Innkeeper? Brian, you're crazy!"

"That's the second time in two days I've been told that; it must be true. But the fact is, I'm unemployed, except for my final job for Goodlin, and I thought we could use that as a honeymoon. Oregon is a great place to take pictures. What do you say?"

"Innkeeper," she muttered softly.

Brian tugged on a strand of her hair. "I've been practicing with Gus; he really thinks I'm good. I have some new ideas for using space, and some promotion deals, and—"

"Brian, stop!" She pressed her fingers lightly over his mouth. "You're a financial genius. An investment whiz. You negotiate big deals. You'd be miserable behind a pine desk in a small town."

"Sydney," he said softly, "you've been so worried about the inn, you've missed something. I've been doing some heavy-duty thinking while wandering around these hills. And I've come to love it here. At first I thought it was just you—that incredible attraction, and then the joy you filled me with—but I realized somewhere along the line it was also what you were helping me to see. I hadn't stopped long enough in a whole lot of years to breathe, Sydney. I breathed here, and a crazy thing happened. I enjoyed it."

"You did?"

Sydney's surprised, delighted smile filled him with happiness. He rocked her body closer to his.

"I do." Brian kissed her gently, then quickly withdrew. The fire in his loins needed little encouragement, and he wanted to get everything out without interruption. He inhaled deeply and placed his hands on her shoulders, turning her around to look out the window. "See that clump of pine near the roll of the land out there?"

She nodded, unsure what would come next; but her concern was minimal as long as Brian stayed only a breath away.

"I want to build a house out there—white, just like Candlewick, and with a sweeping front porch—" One hand moved through the air in front of them. "A house for us—you and me and our children. And at the end of the west wing of the inn—" he pointed toward the far corners of the rambling structure "—I want us to knock down a few walls and build an apartment for Hortense and Tiny, big enough for all her knickknacks and small enough so we can keep an eye on each other."

She lifted her shoulder to bring the hand resting on it to her cheek. She kissed it softly. "I love you even if you're crazy."

"While I have the lady's attention, then—" he wrapped her back into his arms "—there's one more thing."

"You want to turn the library into an investment office."

"No, the tiny office behind the desk. I've been doing a little scouting, and a lot of the fellows around here could use some help in investing their maple-syrup money and the gains from businesses."

"But the innkeeping..."

"Hey," he turned her head with one finger crooked lightly beneath her chin, "I watch *Newhart*. If he can have a television show and run an inn, Hennesy can have some fun in the back room. Where's your faith?"

"Right here." She slipped one hand behind his neck and pulled his head down, pressing her kiss deeply into him.

"I love you," he whispered back, lifting himself from the window seat. "Come here."

He drew her up and into his arms, then half carried her the few feet to the high four-poster and laid her gently on the sun-faded quilt. She watched him through love-dazed eyes as he slipped out of his jacket and dropped it on the chair. And then her eyes closed briefly as she pulled back on the mighty waves of desire.

She opened them as the mattress tilted and gravity drew her to his side. They lay there briefly, their bodies warmed by streams of sunshine and a great calm touching them.

Brian's hands slipped beneath her blouse, and Sydney sighed beneath the gentle downward strokes.

"I nearly forgot," Brian murmured, looking toward the bedside table. "See that lamp?"

Sydney took a steadying breath and looked over his shoulder. "Oh, Brian, it's the one I was looking for, isn't it? It's from Grams's honeymoon."

He nodded. "Gus and I found it. We can give it to her as a wedding remembrance."

Sydney leaned into his fingers and kissed him with new passion. "You're as soft as melted marshmallows, you know that?"

"Uh-huh," he said, slipping his hand out and unbuttoning her blouse. His breath was coming in shallow spurts. "I...think tradition is very important."

Sydney's hand moved toward his belt buckle. "Okay," she whispered. "We'll have lots of traditions." Desire speared through her fiercely.

"Good," he said raggedly, his mouth covering hers after they'd torn off their remaining clothes and their bodies were pressed frantically together. "Then...there's...just... one...more...thing...."

"What?" Sydney breathed with difficulty.

"What...do you think—" he slid his body to hers "—of...a first child...being called...Candlewick?"

But the sounds of love blocked out an answer. And only time would tell.

* * * * *

TALES OF THE RISING MOON
A Desire trilogy by Joyce Thies

MOON OF THE RAVEN—June
Conlan Fox was part American Indian and as tough as the Montana land he rode, but it took fragile yet strong-willed Kerry Armstrong to make his dreams come true.

REACH FOR THE MOON—August
It would take a heart of stone for Steven Armstrong to evict the woman and children living on his land. But when Steven met Samantha, eviction was the last thing on his mind!

GYPSY MOON—October
Robert Armstrong met Serena when he returned to his ancestral estate in Connecticut. Their fiery temperaments clashed from the start, but despite himself, Rob was falling under the Gypsy's spell.

Don't miss any of Joyce Thies's enchanting
TALES OF THE RISING MOON,
coming to you from Silhouette Desire.

SD 432

ATTRACTIVE, SPACE SAVING BOOK RACK

Display your most prized novels on this handsome and sturdy book rack. The hand-rubbed walnut finish will blend into your library decor with quiet elegance, providing a practical organizer for your favorite hard-or soft-covered books.

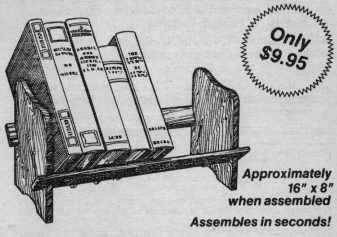

Only $9.95

Approximately 16" x 8" when assembled

Assembles in seconds!

To order, rush your name, address and zip code, along with a check or money order for $10.70* ($9.95 plus 75¢ postage and handling) payable to *Silhouette Books.*

Silhouette Books
Book Rack Offer
901 Fuhrmann Blvd.
P.O. Box 1396
Buffalo, NY 14269-1396

Offer not available in Canada.

BKR-2A

*New York and Iowa residents add appropriate sales tax.

Silhouette Intimate Moments

Rx: One Dose of

DODD
MEMORIAL
HOSPITAL

In sickness and in health the employees of Dodd Memorial Hospital
stick together, sharing triumphs and defeats, and sometimes their
hearts as well. Revisit these special people this month in the new-
est book in Lucy Hamilton's Dodd Memorial Hospital Trilogy, *After
Midnight*—IM #237, the time when romance begins.

Thea Stevens knew there was no room for a man in her life—she
had a young daughter to care for and a demanding new job as the
hospital's media coordinator. But then Luke Adams walked through
the door, and everything changed. She had never met a man like
him before—handsome enough to be the movie star he was, yet
thoughtful, considerate and absolutely determined to get the one
thing he wanted—Thea.

Finish the trilogy in July with *Heartbeats*—IM #245.

 Silhouette Desire

COMING NEXT MONTH

#427 ALONG CAME JONES—Dixie Browning
Tallulah Lavender was a pillar of society. Could she throw over a lifetime of dedication to others for a tall, tough rock-slide of a man? She hesitated . . . then along came Jones!

#428 HE LOVES ME, HE LOVES ME NOT—Katherine Granger
Her book was number one, but Delta Daniels nibbled while she worked—the bestselling diet guru was as fat as a blimp! Enter fitness instructor Kyle Frederick, who aroused other, more compelling appetites. . . .

#429 FORCE OF HABIT—Jacquelyn Lennox
That unprincipled man! Health editor Tara Ross refused to let herself fall for sexy Ethan Boone of Logan Tobacco. Still, she couldn't ignore the spark of passion between them.

#430 TO TAME THE WIND—Sara Chance
Jade Hendricks was as wild and elusive as the animals Russ Blackwell trained. Was his love strong enough to tame her restless heart and set her spirit free?

#431 CAN'T SAY NO—Sherryl Woods
Blake Marshall didn't give Audrey Nelson a chance to say no when he literally swept her off her feet and into his balloon. But would she say yes to love?

#432 MOON OF THE RAVEN—Joyce Thies
The first of three *Tales of the Rising Moon*. One look at ranch foreman Conlan Fox, and Kerry Armstrong knew she'd do anything to win the man of her dreams.

AVAILABLE NOW: